The Beac

JT Harding

Copyright © 2011 by JT Harding

All rights reserved. No part of this publication may be reproduced, stored in a retrieval system, or transmitted, in any form or by any means, electronic, mechanical, photocopying, recording or otherwise without the prior permission of the copyright holder.

All the characters in this book are fictitious, and any resemblance to actual persons, living or dead, is purely coincidental.

Also available on Kindle by JT Harding

Georgia's English Rose
June Bug

Visit JT Harding's website at
http://www.jt-harding.com

For M – she knows who she is

Chapter 1

Jenni Adams parked her rusted pickup behind the Harper house and killed the engine, sat at the wheel as an east wind brought rain over the steep shingle roof and drove it hard against the windshield. The surf would be big today and she anticipated a fight getting through the waves. She wanted this moment to last, sitting perfectly still, letting the urge to swim build inside, the anticipation almost sexual. For Jenni, a lot of things were almost sexual.

She considered her life, her future, and whether a place existed for the couple staying in the beach house next door. She needed to decide two things – hell, at *least* two, she thought, but let's get those nailed down to start.

The first was a biggie. She believed the time had come for her to give serious consideration to leaving her husband.

By comparison, the second was easy. Which of the two people staying in the beach house did she want to make love with most? And then, with a shiver: why not both?

Neither question came with any easy answer. She had been here before, nagging away at what to do about her marriage, like a tongue probing a sore tooth and with pretty much the same result. Leave well alone; worrying only makes the pain worse. Except now the marriage, like an ignored tooth, was reaching a point where she *had* to do something. As for the couple next door, the couple with the baby… Well, she guessed that was mostly wishful thinking.

Jenni had come to the beach to swim, same as she did nearly every day of the year, summer or winter. September came and the Harpers returned home, letting Jenni know the house was hers to use whenever she wanted. She would drive over the spine of the island from town and park on the rough sand and grass strip behind the house, change into her swimwear, then use the electric shower indoors when she returned from the ocean. Even though Kate and Tim were good friends, even though they said use the place whenever she liked, some faint guilt touched her each time because this was their house. She felt like an intruder; although less of one now than she had, after what happened two years before.

***

It had been a warmer day back then when Jenni arrived early at the row of beach houses, as she did every Saturday during summer. Late July, the height of the vacation season, with all six of the houses occupied. At a quarter before seven the sand stretched clean and empty, washed by last night's tide, not yet disturbed by kids with spades and buckets, dry bathers with sun loungers, teenagers making scratch games of beach volleyball scuffing up the surface, or a hundred footprints from people wandering with nowhere particular to be. The sun struggled to clear the fog which still blanketed the edge of the ocean, overhead the sky cloudless. Jenni knew this would change in the afternoon as heat built over the land and cumulus began popping. She sniffed, tasting the air. No rain today.

Jenni parked her pickup behind the last but one house. Kate and Tim Harper had owned it for as long as she remembered. At one time the house had been filled with kids and laughter, the smell of sun oil, drying swimwear and toast – someone was always making toast.

Now the kids had grown and some had kids of their own. Kate and Tim continued to arrive each summer, retired now and with time on their hands. They asked Jenni to use the place out of season, from early September on, their offer mostly but not completely altruistic because Jenni kept the place aired and clean. The houses were let until the end of November, a couple of them all year for those hardy souls craving wild winds and gray skies who didn't mind freezing their butts off for the sake of fresh air, exercise and deserted sand.

September through March was quiet, the beach undisturbed, and Jenni came down to change in the house, as a base to swim for an hour or more a day and a chance to escape her home life. When the sea grew too cold to swim in her bikini

– the one created from visitor cast offs, the top skimpy black nylon too small for her breasts, the bottom mismatched gray lycra in a different style, cut square like boy shorts – she wore the even older wetsuit someone had thrown out and Jenni retrieved after they vacated the house. The wetsuit had a rip on one shoulder, the seams starting to part, but the application of gaffer tape worked wonders, keeping her warm enough to continue swimming right through winter. The Gulf Stream helped as well.

Today the Harper's were in residence. When Kate heard Jenni's pickup still its noisy rattle she came out on the porch and waved.

"Coffee's fresh if you want some, Jen."

Jenni started dragging the first of the laundry bags from the back of the pickup, checked blue and white nylon, each containing fresh sheets and towels for one of the houses. She tugged the Harper's bag off the back of the truck and let it drop to the ground, dragged it around to the steps leading to the porch.

"I'll take you up on the coffee," Jenni said, putting her back into pulling the bag up the three wide steps between beach and porch.

"Hang on, Jen, I'll get Paul to help you."

Paul?

"I can manage."

"I know you can, but you don't have to. Come up here."

Jenni stopped struggling and stepped up onto the porch, tall and lean, the morning sun caught her sun bleached auburn hair, cast light into her dark steel gray eyes. Kate Harper pulled the screen door open and called inside. "Paul, come out here and bring our laundry up."

A muffled reply sounded and a moment later a boy came out. Jenni stared at him, appreciating his perfect young beauty. Dressed only in swim shorts his flat stomach rippled with underlying muscle. No hair showed on his chest, his chin clean shaven, hair straw blond and not far from the same texture, thick and unruly. His blue eyes sparked as he smiled at Kate Harper, the smile stopping short when he caught sight of Jenni and he flushed.

"This is Jenni Adams," Kate made introductions. "She works the houses along this stretch, but I prefer to think of her as my friend." Kate slipped her arm around Jenni's waist and gave a hug.

Jenni smiled, unable to stop herself. She had known Kate so long she felt the same way.

"This is Paul," Kate said. "My grandson. Barbara's eldest. You remember Barbara, don't you?"

Jenni grinned, nodding. "Of course I do." Paul had inherited his mother's blonde hair, although as Jenni recalled Babs' hair had been fine and silky. Barbara had been Jenni's first crush, twelve years old, hormones starting to kick in and Barbara had been nice to her. Nice, and with a killer figure and the face of an angel. Jenni offered her hand, and after a moment's hesitation Paul took four steps across the porch and shook hers, pulling away almost as soon as their fingers met, as though her touch had transferred an electric shock. His blush deepened and he nodded stiffly. Young men, Jenni thought – you just gotta love 'em.

"Great to meet you, Paul."

"Pleased to meet you too." Paul spoke without looking at her. "Is this the stuff you want fetching up, Gram?" He took the steps in one long jump and gripped the carry handles on the laundry bag, relieved to take the offered escape.

"In the back room please, Paul."

He lifted the bag easily and Jenni let herself admire the way muscle bunched in his back and shoulders, how his thighs popped hard as he lifted. He slung the bag over his shoulder and pushed through the door.

"Take the weight off, Jen." Kate poured a large mug of coffee, pushed cream and sugar across the faded wooden table. Jenni added both and sat in a pale chair and sipped, enjoying the aroma and taste. Kate made the best coffee on the island.

"I can't believe he's all grown, Kate. Last time I saw Babs she was what, twenty-four, twenty-five, and he must have been two, three years old?" Jenni retrieved an image of Kate's pretty daughter, long blonde hair and good figure, a small round boy on stocky legs marching up and down the beach with buckets of water holding crabs, which his Mom made him take right back.

"I guess," Kate said. "You can't have been much more than twelve yourself."

Jenni laughed. "No, I guess not. Where does the time go, Kate?"

Kate returned the laugh. "Tell me. Just wait until you get to my age."

The screen door opened and her husband came out on the porch.

"Hey, Jen, I didn't know you were here." Tim Harper was still lean at seventy, with a full head of hair now turned completely white. The first time Jenni met him his hair had been dark brown and he wore a mustache; but that was the late eighties for you, and Jenni had been about five, accompanying her mother who had done this job before her.

"How's it hanging, Tim?" Jenni asked, and he laughed at the usual greeting, laughed as he did every time.

"Same as ever, though sad to say a little less every year."

"Tim!" Kate wasn't as shocked as she sounded, smiling as she always did, accustomed to the innocent flirting that went on between Jenni and her husband.

As if emboldened by the presence of his grandfather Paul returned to the porch, the screen door slapping back against the wall once more. He leaned against the railing on the far side of the table, trying for casual but succeeding only in looking sexy as all hell. Or so Jenni thought.

"You swimming later?" Tim asked her.

"What do you think, old timer?"

He laughed. "I guess you are. God, I wish I was still young enough to keep up with you, Jen."

"You still could, I reckon."

"Maybe, maybe not."

Jenni tried to remember the exact time they had started playing these little games. Probably there had been no first time, only a slow shift in their relationship. She would be horrified if she thought Tim really meant anything, but the game was fun, nothing more, Kate playing along as much as her husband, giving them all satisfaction.

"Paul swims," Kate said. "He swims for his school."

"Not anymore, Gram," Paul said, his first words since coming back out, though he still refused to look across at Jenni.

"No, of course not. I forgot. He's going to college in the Fall, Jen."

"Where?" Jenni asked, interested. She liked to hear about people bettering themselves. She might have wanted that for herself, but too late now. Twenty-seven and settled into a miserable marriage with a loser husband and no obvious way out. Still, she enjoyed other people's success, other people's escape.

"Cal Tech," he said, staring at the beach as though something important lay on the sand, something only he could see.

"That's a long way from home."

"No, Jen. Barbara lives in San Jose now," Kate said. "I'm sure I told you."

Jenni laughed. "You probably did, Kate, but you know I can never remember anything like that. So how good are you, Paul?"

"Good?" He finally glanced in her direction.

"In the water. Think you can beat me?"

She caught him suppressing a smile. "Guess so." He didn't seem impressed by the challenge.

Tim Harper laughed and slapped his grandson on the shoulder. "Don't make promises you can't deliver on, boy. You've never seen Jen in the water."

"I reckon I can still beat her." Paul straightened up, turned his head to glance at Jenni. He was tall and lean in the way swimmers are, and Jenni tried and failed to stop her glance skittering down to the respectable bulge in his swim shorts. She hoped he didn't catch where her eyes went, because if he did it would be her turn to blush.

"A challenge, I think, don't you Jen?" Tim asked.

"A definite challenge."

"Race–race–race," Tim chanted.

"Grampa!"

"Not till I've finished the houses," Jenni said.

Paul had worked his courage up and looked directly at her. He was so damn beautiful, so sexy, Jenni hoped the tingle stiffening her nipples did not betray her lust.

"You really want to race?" Paul asked.

Jenni nodded. "Sure. I'll be done by two, three at the latest."

Tim Harper laughed. "You've gone and done it now, boy. Done it good."

Paul looked at his grandfather, the affection obvious in his glance. "We'll see."

Jenni finished her coffee and allowed Paul to drag the bag containing the dirty laundry round to her truck. He hoisted the bag up with the same easy pull of his shoulders as before and Jenni glanced away, knowing the thoughts bubbling in her mind about this youth were entirely inappropriate. How old was he anyway? Too young for the thoughts filling her head. Seventeen if he was just out of high school. God, how could she even think about him that way?

She knew what was wrong, the same thing as always. She possessed a vast sex drive with nowhere to express it. Her husband, only ever moderately ardent, took marriage as a signal to stop trying altogether. A week after the church service what little libido he may once have possessed melted to nothing.

Jenni had no outlet for her needs, not on an island as small as this where everyone knew everyone else. She had enjoyed some liaisons in the past, but all vacation people. A forty year old husband showed interest, and Jenni experienced no guilt when she let him fuck her senseless, lying out on the dunes the night before he vacated his rental. But Jenni drew the line at an underage conquest, however beautiful.

Paul pushed the tailgate closed, squealing its usual protest.

"Grampa said I should come help you with the rest." He stared down at his feet. "I told him you probably wouldn't want me tagging along." He glanced up, caught her looking at him and his eyes darted away. "Do you?"

"I could do with the help," Jenni said, amused. Maybe she couldn't jump his bones, but that didn't prevent her appreciating his beauty. She would enjoy teasing him some too. That might be fun. "Only if you haven't got anything else planned. There are some kids your age in the Bradley place this week. Have you met them?"

"They're only sixteen." Paul's tone was dismissive.

"Ah, of course." Jenni tried to keep the smile from her face. "Come on then, if you're going to help climb aboard." She pulled herself up behind the wheel and turned the clunky engine over. Paul came round and sat across from her.

"I'm eighteen Tuesday," he said, obviously trying to make his voice casual.

"You are?" Jenni turned in the seat, peering through the mottled rear window as she backed out, knowing the movement was pushing her breasts tight against the t-shirt, knowing Paul's eyes would be on her tits. She suppressed that smile again. It felt good to tease him, even if she didn't plan on going any further. "You having a party?"

She bullied the gearshift into first, crawled the pickup around the house and along the beach to the next a hundred yards further on. Later she would work her way back, after everyone had either left for the ferry ride to the mainland or gone out for the day, cleaning each house in turn.

"Mom threw me a big party back home before I flew out," Paul said. "Gramps said we might have a small one Tuesday, just the three of us, as it'll be my real birthday."

"No girls from, you know…" Jenni nodded toward the Bradley house on the end of the row.

"They're a bit immature." Paul stared out the window as though the surf was the most fascinating thing he had ever seen.

Jenni laughed. "Yeah, I guess they might seem that way to an almost eighteen year old."

She saw Paul glance at her, not sure if she was making fun of him or not. His look sent a thrill all the way along her spine. No, she thought, not making fun of him… not making fun of him at all.

Chapter 2

The day was edging toward a close as Jenni walked from the sea in her mismatched bikini. Her body tingled from expended energy, the pleasure heightened by the drubbing she had given Paul. He might be a good swimmer, but Jenni swam at least an hour every day of the year and only someone outstanding was going to beat her, particularly on the long half mile route she had set. She heard Paul trailing along behind, his breathing still coming fast. She twirled back and laughed.

"Don't sweat it, honey; no-one's beaten me yet."

He grinned and she liked there was no rancor in him. "Next year," he said.

"You coming back next year? Think you can handle more humiliation?"

"I'm coming back so I can beat you." His grin widened, eyes meeting Jenni's, not as afraid of her as he had been.

At Kate's house Jenni used the cold shower out back to wash the salt off before changing in the lean-to shed. She heard the shower running indoors, right next to the wall the shed was built against. Her mind projected the few feet through the shingles to imagine Paul standing under the shower, water cascading over his lean body. She wondered if his cock was hard in the same way as her nipples, wondered if he was rubbing himself and for a moment lust filled her body, making her weak. She had dried but not dressed, stood with one hand against the wall while the other crept down, touched her belly and slid lower. Jenni adjusted her stance, opening her legs to admit her fingers, touching herself, cold from the sea but as she pushed her fingers inside they were met by warmth and a smooth slickness.

She gasped, aroused, her eyes fluttering shut. Through the wall she sensed, or imagined she sensed, the faint vibration made by the shower. The sound stopped. Jenni stood alone, fingers thrust inside herself, ashamed of the thoughts in her head. Paul might be about to turn eighteen, but still so young. She withdrew her fingers and dressed, hoping to cover her arousal.

When she emerged carrying the two mismatched parts of her wet bikini in her hand it was Jenni who avoided Paul's gaze as he came on the porch toweling his hair dry, dressed in blue jeans and a sweatshirt.

"Are you swimming tomorrow?" Paul's eyes locked on hers and a thrill coursed through Jenni. He had become more adventurous, bolder.

"I swim every day."

"I'll probably catch you then, if you don't mind some company."

"Don't mind company."

Jenni drove back over the island into town. As she came down the hill a ferry was docking, bringing more visitors, ready to return day-trippers to the mainland. The ferry, regular as any clock, said a few minutes after five and Mark would be home by six wanting his evening meal, would likely be out again by seven drinking with his buddies. At least it meant he wouldn't be home. Jenni preferred it when she had the house to herself, ever since Mark started taking his frustration at life out on her. Nothing much to begin with, words and shouting at the start, then a year ago the physical stuff began, a light slap, a punch to the ribs. What worried her was the escalation. Sometimes Mark didn't seem aware just how hard he hit her.

Had she allowed herself to imagine an escape, had some feasible option existed, she was starting to think she might take it, wondering how long it was going to be before *any* other option was better than the one she had accepted.

***

Sunday Jenni beat Paul, same again on Monday, but he was catching on to her style, getting closer each day. Or perhaps she was letting him get closer. Her resolution of Saturday not to think about him sexually had blown to the winds; she couldn't *stop* thinking about him, conjuring fantasies of his tight young body, picturing him naked, picturing what she wanted to do with him.

Tuesday morning when Mark left for work Jenni showered and after she dried stood naked in front of the tall bathroom mirror. She leaned forward to wipe the steam stippled surface, stared at her distorted body appearing slowly as the air cooled and the mirror cleared.

She turned sideways, put her hand on her flat belly, examining herself. Like many women Jenni accomplished that dichotomy of thought more common than each individual realized. In private she considered herself hot, in public believing her looks less than average. Perhaps because of the way people treated her. Looking at herself, her high breasts self-supporting despite their size, her lean belly and long legs, the neat tuft of hair covering her sex, she considered she looked pretty good. Jenni knew in company her confidence would leach away, eroded by Mark's words and actions. She resolved to dismiss all doubts, dismiss the years of verbal abuse which had grown so endemic she hardly noticed the constant denigration. Looking at herself in the mirror she allowed herself to believe in her beauty.

Jenni turned again, twisting to stare over her shoulder, noticing the way skin tightened along her side, outlining the lower ribs. Good ass, she thought, round and tight, narrow hips and slim thighs. A horizontal ledge showed between her legs and she leaned forward, putting her palms flat on the floor, shocked at the wave of arousal crashing through her as she stared back between her legs at full pussy lips, shivering at the sight and knowing she was not doing herself any favors.

Turning herself on was going to get her exactly nowhere other than back on the bed with her hand between her legs. Temptation whispered in her ear, and on another day she might have given in. She frequently resorted to pleasuring herself, at least every other day. Mark seemed not to care about sex anymore, and when he did the act was always short and brutish, often as not accompanied by acts of minor violence.

Today was different and Jenni knew the reason why. Today was Paul's birthday. Today he turned eighteen, and although

Jenni acknowledged her thoughts were foolish she couldn't help wondering if there wasn't something she had to offer him. Foolish, because absolutely nothing – *nothing* – was going to happen. The hopeless fantasy warmed her, making her wet between the legs, and she nourished that warmth, allowing the arousal to seep through her body, stiffening her nipples and bringing a flush to her neck.

Tuesday through Friday were good days, quiet days when she would go to the beach and check everyone had what they needed, nothing was broken or damaged, ask if anyone needed help or advice. Dressed in cut off denims and a tank top, her mismatched bikini worn beneath, a change of underclothes in the pickup, she parked behind the Harper house at eleven. As she came around the side she found them on the porch. Paul had his long legs up on the railing, binoculars to his face. Kate and Tim drank coffee, working their way slowly through a pile of fresh chocolate brownies.

"Hey, Jen, come and have a birthday brownie."

She laughed. "I don't want to spoil the party."

"Since when could you ever spoil anything," Kate said. "Come up here. Paul, get Jenni a coffee."

Paul dropped his legs off the rail and went inside. He came back a minute later with a plain white mug billowing good fresh coffee aroma. The smell hit Jenni and she had no choice but to sit and savor.

"How's the swimming," she said to Paul. "Think you can beat me now you're an adult?" She held his gaze, trying to communicate something even though she wasn't exactly sure what message she was trying to send.

"Oh yeah, I'm so much older than when you beat me yesterday."

"You're going to try though."

"What do you think?"

She sipped her coffee and nodded. "I think you are."

"Are you swimming now?" Kate asked. "Because Tim and I need to go into town after lunch, so if you're going to stay for the birthday lunch as well, Jen, you'd better swim now."

"We can always do both, Grams," Paul said. "Before and

after lunch. Once Jenni's tired I might stand some sort of a chance."

"In your dreams, young 'un." Jenni laughed. She saw Paul smile, a secret inner smile, and it sent a shiver through her.

"I think they forgot to buy anything for my birthday," Paul said, "so they've got to go into town and find something quick."

"You won't be quick if you're looking for a present in town," Jenni said. "Or maybe you will, because there's not much!"

"We have something we need to do," Tim said, his face pleasant but closed.

"Let's go humiliate you then," Jenni said. "Again."

Paul grinned and stood up, stretching his muscles. Jenni went round the back and stripped her denims and tank top off and walked back to the bottom of the porch.

"Why don't you let me give you one of my old suits, Jen?" Kate asked. "I don't use them now, and I'm sure they would fit you."

Jenni shook her head, long tresses brushing her shoulders. "This is my lucky outfit, Kate. If I change it now Paul might beat me."

"We can't have that," Kate said.

They walked down to the line of surf. Families, kids, teenagers and old folks dotted the sand, sun loungers arrayed, each one an unspoken but understood and accepted distance for the others. Balls bounced, kids yelled, romances sparked. Jenni glimpsed the sixteen year old girls from the Bradley house talking with two boys their own age. Jenni guessed Paul had missed his chance, despite his protests he wasn't interested. The girls were cute in tiny bathing suits, white zinc on their pretty noses.

When their swim was over and they returned from the water the sun said midday, Paul laughing because Jenni had beaten him again, but only by twenty yards.

"I'll get you after lunch," he said. "You're staying for my birthday lunch, aren't you?"

"I'm not sure I should, Paul. You ought to be spending your birthday with family."

"I am. But I'd like if you stayed as well." He slowed and when Jenni turned her head it was to see him staring hard at her, staring into her eyes as they met his, and the flutter started up in her belly and she wondered if Paul noticed her nipples suddenly peak against her top.

"I'll think about it," she said, knowing the argument, if one ever existed, was already lost.

She showered and changed, pulling clean underwear over her still damp body and when she knocked on the door and went in the table was laid with fish, mango salsa, fruit, bottles of wine beaded with moisture, and a small chocolate birthday cake decorated with eighteen unlit candles. As soon as they finished eating Tim put a match against each candle and placed the cake in the center of the table.

"All at once," he said. "Then you get to make a wish."

Paul leaned over the table and blew. He blew long and hard until every candle was extinguished. He closed his eyes and kept them shut for half a minute.

"Some wish!" Tim said.

Paul opened his eyes, blushing, glanced shyly at Jenni. "Might as well make it worthwhile. I'm only going to be eighteen once, even if this is my second party."

"Ah, youth," Tim sighed.

"Okay," Kate said. "Let's clear up then we really have to scoot."

"We'll do this, Grams." Paul glanced at Jenni. "If that's okay with you?"

"Do you mind, Jen?" Kate asked. "It doesn't seem right asking you to a party and then letting you and the birthday boy clean up, but we could use the extra time in town."

"Sure, no problem." Something had loosened inside Jenni over lunch. Perhaps two glasses of wine had something to do with it, perhaps something else, but her skin tingled with anticipation. She was, she reminded herself, only seven years older than this young man. Okay, maybe eight years; but eight years was nothing.

As his grandparents drove away Jenni helped Paul stack dishes in the machine, knowing she could not prevent herself instigating the next step. What happened after that was up to Paul.

Chapter 3

Through the kitchen window the beach was quiet. While they had eaten low gray clouds scudded in, discouraging all but the most adventurous. Leaning towards her while Jenni passed the plates Paul asked, "You want another swim later?"

"In a while, maybe. I need to let some of that wine work out of my system first."

"Yeah, probably a good idea. What do you want to do then?"

Fuck your brains out, she thought, but what she said was, "Oh, I'm easy. It's your birthday."

"I don't mind." He finished with the last plate and rose on his toes to stack it in the high cabinet, his body lithe and powerful. He half turned, close now, and Jenni became instantly aroused as his scent enveloped her. Salt and sun oil and something deeply masculine underlying everything.

"I thought I might give you a present," Jenni said, her words soft.

"You don't need to do that." Somehow, although neither of them had moved, the space between had shrunk.

"I want to."

"It doesn't seem right. I hope you didn't spend much."

Jenni smiled. "I didn't spend a thing."

"Oh… okay. What have you got me?"

Jenni took a pace toward him, placed her hands flat against his chest. "This."

She lifted on her toes and pressed her lips against his. For a moment she thought it was a mistake, Paul stunned, or afraid, or shocked, she couldn't tell which and a flare of panic filled her because she was doing the wrong thing. Paul's sudden gasp drew air from her lungs. His firm young body trembled beneath her hands and Jenni stopped worrying she had stepped over the line. His lips parted in response. She had not meant things to go so fast, intending the kiss as a promise for the future, but before she could prevent herself she pressed hard against his chest, her mouth opening, tongue probing. Paul's hand pressed into the curve of her back, pulling her closer, pulling her against his instant arousal pressing her stomach.

The kiss went on and on, changing, Paul pushing past her tongue and between her lips. Jenni dropped her hand to his waist, the slim tightness of muscle along his flank beneath her fingers. She wanted to move her hand lower but hesitated, because this was going fast, maybe too fast. How long did they have? How long could she wait? She knew the answer in an instant. She could not wait at all.

Jenni pulled back, breathing hard. Paul stood as though stunned, the long hard ridge inside his jeans obvious.

Jenni darted back and kissed him again, a fleeting peck this time.

"Happy birthday." She took his hand.

"Uhm."

"Come on," Jenni said, "there's more, if you want." She had moved beyond restraint. Pent-up lust boiled inside her, scorching away any doubt she had. How long, she wondered, as she led Paul through to the living room, how long before his grandparents returned? She had the impression they might be gone a while. Perhaps they had planned it this way.

Jenni led Paul by the hand, his features slack with disbelief, a dream state on his handsome face. Jenni drew him to the sofa and pushed him back on the cushions, straddled him and kissed him again, her hands holding his face and after a moment his hands slid along her back and clasped her. She ground her hips against him, the hardness inside his jeans pressing back, offering a promise she intended to fulfill. Her cut-off denims allowed the nakedness of her thighs to rest against Paul's jeans, filling her with a sensual longing. She wanted to feel his skin against hers.

Jenni dropped her hands, pulling at the buttons on his shirt, opening them and slipping her fingers inside, her fingertips experiencing his hard smoothness. She kissed his neck, put her hands on her own tank top and drew it up. Jenni watched Paul's eyes widen as she revealed her breasts cupped inside a small white bra, their nipples hard, peaking against the lace.

"Touch me," Jenni's voice a whisper. When Paul failed to respond she took his hands and lifted them to her breasts, gasping as his palms closed over them. "Like this, touch me like this."

She returned to his buttons until his shirt gaped wide, leaned and kissed his neck, moved lower and nipped at his nipple with her teeth. Men were sensitive and got hard there too, and she licked and sucked at him as he jerked between her lips.

His hands grew bolder against her breasts, probing, pushing down inside the cup of her bra, searching for and finding her nipples. Jenni reached behind and flicked a clasp and the bra fell away, granting Paul's hands full access. She arched her back, presenting herself to him, rewarded when his mouth closed around her nipple. His tongue caressed the stiff nub and sensation arced through her, a direct line drawn from nipple to clitoris. Paul, she decided, still had too many clothes on.

Jenni allowed him to suck on her nipples, as a reward, and also because his lips were so good against her breast, then she pulled away, slipping down to the floor between his legs. She put her hands on the brass clip of his jeans and looked up at him, asking the question without forming words, and Paul gave the merest nod. Jenni twisted the clasp, slowly popping each brass button along his fly, her eyes devouring the sight revealed. When all the buttons were loose she tugged at his jeans and Paul lifted his hips, allowing her to pull them down. His shorts caught and came with them, not all the way, only as far as the base of his pubic hair, the root of his hard cock showing.

Jenni kissed his hip, his belly, placed her hand directly over the long shape formed by his cock and Paul gasped.

"Oh Jesus, I'm going to have an accident if you do that."

"Not an accident," Jenni said her voice hoarse. She tugged at his shorts, wanting to see all of him, wanting to taste him. He lifted again and his cock worked free, slapping back hard against his belly. Jenni grasped him, impressed at the length and thickness of his cock, impressed at the hard smoothness. She stroked him once and saw him twitch. Oh yes, accident on the way, a delicious accident. She had no idea how this felt for him but she could guess. He would be on a hair trigger now, trying to hold himself back and about to fail. Jenni determined to make him fail.

She leaned forward and put her mouth against the side of his cock, licked the smooth hot skin and he twitched again.

"No, no," he gasped, but Jenni was relentless. She shifted upward and her lips found the head of his cock and closed around his glans, pulling him inside her mouth. The taste of his cock was sweet against her tongue, the head slick with pre-cum. Paul tried to hold her head and pull her away but she knocked his hands aside.

"I want to do this." Freeing her mouth only long enough to say the words.

"You're gonna make me come," he cried, anguish in his voice.

"Good."

"But..."

"It's okay, honey, I want you to. I want you to come in my mouth."

Jenni took him back between her lips, deeper this time, she had always given good head, had a reputation at one time she hated, but now she *knew* she gave good head, wished her husband wanted her to do this to him, knowing he was a lost cause. Instead she would enjoy the pleasure of this afternoon. This beautiful boy with his long, thick cock was all hers.

"Ahh!" Paul cried out, and Jenni pressed down, his cock touching the top of her throat and pressing down again so he filled her. She pulled back at the moment he tipped over, unable to prevent himself, his hips jerking upward and the first explosion of sweet slickness filled her mouth and she accepted his offering, swallowing what she could but he jerked too much and pulled free of her lips, spurting enormous arcing jets of semen which caught in her hair, splashed against her face, spattered across her breasts and he came again and again and again, the fecundity of his youth covering Jenni in cum.

She grabbed his cock and drew him back against her tongue, ignoring his gasp. Still rock hard, still rigid, still ready.

She played with his glans, explored the tip of his cock with her tongue, moved up and kissed his belly, his chest, coming finally to his mouth and kissing him, her bare breasts smearing semen against his chest.

"Oh God, I'm sorry," he said, speaking against her mouth.

"Sorry for what?"

"Coming like that."

"Why?"

"I should have lasted longer."

"Why?" Jenni rolled to lie beside him, circling his cock with her fingers. "You're still hard."

He turned to her. "Do you want to…" he stopped, shy.

"I want to do everything, Paul." Jenni kissed a point on his neck below the ear.

"I want to make you come now," he said, avoiding her eyes.

"Really?"

He nodded, before realizing she was teasing, smiled. "I do."

"I guess I could let you, if you really want to," Jenni said.

His eyes widened, as though he had not expected that answer. "How… what… can I…" He shook his head, lost for words.

"Anything," Jenni said. "Everything."

"I don't know what…"

"Paul, have you ever done this before? With a woman? A girl?"

He both nodded and shook his head at the same time, his head making a crazy circle. "Yeah. Kind of. Once. Sort of."

"Good. Tell me, what did you do?" Jenni drew close to him, fascinated by his skin, his lean strength. She caressed his cock, stroked his balls, round and still so full of potential. She wanted all of him. She dipped down and sucked his cock into her mouth again, but only for a moment. "Has anyone ever done this to you before?"

He nodded. "Once. But she didn't want me to do anything… in her mouth."

"Did you do the same for her?"

He shook his head. "She didn't want me to… "

"Huh. Silly girl." Jenni took him back inside, but only to

tease, to keep him on edge. She had other plans. "You taste good."

"I do?"

Jenni rolled along his body and kissed his mouth. "You do. Can't you taste yourself on my mouth?" She kissed him again.

Paul nodded. "I think I can."

"You can," Jenni said. "Have you had sex? Have you fucked a girl?"

Paul shook his head.

"Hand job?"

He nodded.

"What else?" Jenni was turning herself on even more asking him questions, turned on by his innocence and need.

"Boobs," he said.

"You fucked her boobs?" Jenni was delighted.

Paul nodded.

"You splashed on them?"

He nodded again, looking away.

"You want to try again?"

He looked down at her breasts, full and soft, nodded.

"I want you to do something else too."

"What kind of thing?"

Jenni rolled on her back and unclipped her denims, pushed them down, displaying skimpy white panties, the front showing evidence of her arousal.

"You can fuck me, Paul, if you want. No – I *want* you to fuck me. You *have* to fuck me. But only after you've done something else first."

"Anything," he said, staring at the mound her pussy made in her panties, at the stray curls of pubic hair working free around the sides.

"Can you guess what I want?" Jenni asked.

He continued to stare at her panties, nodding slowly. "I think so."

"Have you ever gone down on a girl, Paul?" Jenni was arousing herself with the words she spoke to him, stimulated by her boldness.

He shook his head.

"Girls love it when you do that."

"They never said anything."

"They're not as forward as me. Will you do it for me now, Paul, please?"

He nodded again and slipped to the floor. Jenni parted her knees, his body sliding between to press against her legs. Paul had come fast, but Jenni knew she was going to match him, delight building inside. Paul ran his hand along her thigh, his fingers shying away from her pussy. She grabbed Paul's hand and moved his fingers back where she wanted, pressing herself directly onto them.

"Take my panties off, honey," she said.

He tugged the skimpy cotton, a wave of heat rising against his face as he revealed her sex. Jenni lifted one leg, freeing the panties on one side, letting them hang from her knee on the other.

She put her fingers against her labia and opened her pussy. "Here... I want you right here."

Paul glanced up at her, eyes wide, followed her directions. His breath fluttered warm on her bush. His lips touched her on one side, kissed her like he had kissed her mouth.

"Use your tongue."

Paul pushed between her slit, extending his tongue inside. He was clumsy, unsure what to do, but it was okay because his inexperience excited Jenni and when the tremble started she tried to hold back, not wanting to come yet, wanting to make this last.

"Here," she said, pushing her fingers down beside his face. She pressed against her clitoris, showing him how hard and fat it was protruding from beneath its hood. "Kiss me here, Paul. Girls really like being kissed here."

He moved his attention to the new target, pulled her clitoris between his lips, added his tongue.

"Oh yes, honey... are you sure you haven't done this before?"

"Nn-uhn," he grunted, and Jenni smiled.

"Well, you're gonna make some girls real happy real soon, baby. Real happy."

He pulled her clit deep into his mouth, his fingers joining the mix, pushing a little roughly between her thighs, two fingers entering her and Jenni felt the time arrive when she was incapable of holding back any longer.

"Yeah, go on honey, do me now," she gasped. It had been years since anyone had done this for her. Mark considered the act to be filthy, said more than once he couldn't understand why any man would want to do something as perverted and gross. Paul was doing great though, so good for his first time, so, so good...

Jenni pushed up against his face, pushing hard and fast, riding against his mouth, making his fingers slip and move inside her. She reached down and grabbed his free hand, placed it on her breast, pulled at her other nipple herself as the peak started deep inside and grew fast.

"Oh, yes!" Paul sucked her clitoris harder and faster as she rode against him, for a moment the world spinning away from her, spinning far away before coming back with a bang and she cried out, riding the wave until sated.

Her body went slack, still tremored with twitches and shivers. Jenni grabbed Paul's hair, tugging him up, not caring if she hurt him, pulling him up to kiss her.

"Thanks, honey," she said into his mouth.

"Thank you," he said, the perfect gentleman. "That was... something else."

"It surely was," Jenni said, planting kisses on his lips and cheeks, "and we ain't done yet."

He looked at her. "Are we going to?"

She nodded.

"What about... uh, precautions?"

"All taken care of," she said. After her swim Jenni had taken her cap, the one she rarely used, and inserted the device inside herself.

Paul looked down at her. Jenni reached for his beautiful cock and circled the thick shaft.

"I think I can last a little longer this time," Paul said, and his sudden seriousness made her break up.

"Oh God, honey, I like the sound of that. Come on, I'm

ready." She wrapped her legs around his narrow waist, her hand still on his cock, guiding him to the moistness of her entrance. The thick head of his cock touched her, resting against the engorged lips of her pussy and she pushed against him. Paul wasn't experienced enough to tease, and Jenni didn't want to draw this out. As he entered her Jenni clasped her heels against his back and pulled him deep inside.

She examined his face as he sank into her, watched the way his pupils bloomed. He stared back at her, the shy boy gone, the start of a confident man growing and Jenni experienced a huge wave of affection for him, so glad she could do this for him. Do this for herself as well... probably, she thought, if I'm being honest, mostly for myself.

"Go on," she said. "Hard. I want you to fuck me hard." The coarseness of her words excited them both.

Paul moved against her, working solidly, his cock extending so deep inside she wondered where it reached but still trying to impale herself even harder onto him. Already the urge had blossomed from a pinpoint inside and Jenni knew this was going to be fast again. The pinprick grew as Paul pounded into her. Sweat gathered on his chin and dripped to her breasts. His fists dug into the sofa either side of her waist and she loved the concentration on his face, loved the fact he was close to coming, the idea exciting her even more.

"Fuck me," she whispered, drawing her lips up to his ear. "I want you to fuck me, honey."

She didn't think he could move any faster but somehow he managed and his cock became a constant thrum inside her, touching every nerve ending she had, trembling hard as the joy cascaded through her body.

"Yes," she gasped. "Do me, babe, do me like that..."

He grunted, Jenni ready too, the first spasm erupting and becoming a flood deep inside, tipping her beyond pleasure and into chaos, crying out and gripping his shoulders, biting his arm, jerking and trembling against him, his entire naked body pressed against hers and still she couldn't get enough of him.

When he finally brought her back to reality by drawing away Jenni glanced down to find his cock still hard.

"Do we have time?" he asked.

Jenni rolled over, leaning her arms on the sofa and lifting her ass high into the air.

"This way," she said, and Paul lodged himself between her legs. His hands gripped her waist and confident now he guided himself home, pressing deep between her thighs, his cock once more filling her pussy.

This time was slower, their movements gentler, more loving. The first times had been all wild lust and passion, this was soft and filled with affection. Paul worked himself inside her, a fast learner, his belly slapping against her ass on each stroke, and Jenny reached back and pulled her cheeks apart, knowing she was displaying her asshole to him, wanting to display herself. He stroked her back, touching the valley running along her spine, held her ass, gripping her cheeks tight inside his hands. Jenni pushed back harder, wanting him to do something but not wanting to ask him, shy herself now at what she needed him to do. He leaned over and kissed her back, reached beneath and cradled her breast in his palm, so full she overflowed his hand. He gripped her hips again, working himself deeper. He ran a finger along her spine and down along the crack of her ass and Jenni reached back and parted herself again. His fingertip touched her budded asshole and she twitched.

Jenni felt Paul hesitate as he realized how sensitive this spot was for her. His finger returned and Jenni put her head down and grunted. "Yes, honey... touch me right there." She said the words, spoke them aloud, allowing her need into the open.

Paul touched her again, and this time his finger returned slick with his saliva. He pressed, lightly at first, as though uncertain, but when she offered no resistance the pressure increased and his finger invaded her most taboo of places. As though a signal had been given their slow love making increased in pace. Paul pounded harder and faster. His finger probed deeper into her ass. Jenni pushed back against him, ready again, encouraging him on. She peaked, tipped over and still when she came back he had not come and she thrilled because it wasn't finished, grunting at him, not words but her meaning clear and he pounded harder, his finger popping free of her ass so he could grip both hands on her hips, needing to work harder, deeper, and Jenni heard him breathing hoarsely, the tension in his body peaking and he cried out, emptying inside her again, so young, so much potential, filling her once more and his climax triggered her own and she pressed her curled up fists into the cushions and bit on her bottom lip.

***

It was after five when Kate and Tim returned. The living room was tidy, all the plates and glasses dried and put away, but Jenni feared the house still stank of their lovemaking, would give them both away. Instead of coming inside they called Paul out.

Jenni joined them on the porch, hanging back, and Kate shot her a probing, questioning glance but Jenni kept her expression neutral.

"Happy birthday, Paul." Tim disappeared around the side of the house, appearing a moment later pulling a trolley of some kind. As more came into view a small sailing dinghy emerged, second hand but refurbished, the nylon sail furled tight, all the rigging ready to go.

"What?" Paul's mouth hung open.

Jenni gazed at him, a warm glow tingling inside. This is some birthday, she thought. Her body ached, satisfied; maybe satisfied for another year or two.

"Grams, Grampa, what… this is too much…"

"Well, we thought you might be able to catch Jenni with this," Tim said, and he cast the same questioning glance at her and she wondered if what they had done showed on their faces, in the way they held their bodies. She never did find out if they guessed what had gone on, not for sure.

Paul insisted she go sailing, and she went with him but made him bring her back in time to return home before Mark finished work. Paul stayed another twelve days before he had to fly west, and Jenni met him almost every single one of those days, going out on the water in his neat little dinghy, and each day they sailed far out, as far as Sedge island where they anchored and Jenni taught him other ways to please a woman, showed him what a woman can do for a man.

She feared tears when he left, from her as well as him, but he had matured over these few weeks, and Jenni liked to think she had helped. After he had gone the glow kindled inside by him lasted months. She was convinced Kate and Tim knew, but if they did nothing was ever mentioned, and she never once caught any hint of judgment.

Jenni expected Paul to return the year after, but he didn't turn up. She asked Kate and Tim casually what he was doing, and discovered, over weeks, he had found a girlfriend and it was serious. They were engaged, planned to marry when they finished college. Jenni wasn't sure how she felt about the news. Happy for Paul, but happiness tinged with an undercurrent of jealousy. Then, eventually, she laughed at herself. What had she expected anyway? He was going to come back like a love-torn puppy dog and follow her around forever? She wouldn't have wanted that anyway, would have been scared if something like that happened.

That summer of two years earlier faded. The houses closed up one by one. Winter storms arrived and Jenni's husband withdrew even further into himself. Jenni tried to be a good wife, tried to offer sympathy because she knew things were hard on Mark. He had taken over the small auto-repair business started by his father, and at first everything had gone well. Gradually, over time, Jenni picked up things were getting tougher. New cars needed new equipment to fix them. Mark complained that everything was controlled by computers these days. Foreign crap was forcing out good American cars. He could fix anything built before the turn of the century, but now people were taking their vehicles to the big outfits on the mainland. He was left with the old trucks and cars, Fords and Chryslers he knew all about. He kept his head above water changing tires, topping up oil and selling gas. But it was not clear he would be able to do that for ever. If Mark had confided in her, offered a little more response when she tried to help life might have been different. Instead he retreated into himself, into drink and his buddies, losers all of them but they shared his world view, a small world that encompassed little outside of the island.

Jenni knew another summer would arrive, perhaps bringing another chance to grasp at happiness. This was her life. This was the way it always had been, the way she believed it always would be, and she was learning how to make the best of it.

She had no intimation this summer that was almost over would be different. The young couple staying in the end house with their new baby fascinated her. The woman in particular was hot, something about her radiating sexual energy. Jenni had never experienced sex with another woman, not real sex. She had messed around in high school, everyone had, but something about this woman intrigued her, lighting a spark inside which took her thoughts in strange new directions.

Chapter 4

Joe was standing at the kitchen window drinking a glass of water when Kim came up behind him and slipped her arms round his waist.

"What you looking at, old timer?" Her chin rested against his shoulder, eyes peering above.

"That woman again. The same one I saw yesterday coming out from next door."

"Am I not enough for you anymore?"

Joe pushed his butt back against her, hearing the laugh in her voice. "You know the answer to that. I was curious, that's all."

Kim slid around Joe's body, gaining a better view. The woman was walking out from the ocean, pushing dark hair back from her face. She walked stiffly until her legs were clear of the surf, more elegantly as she reached the wet sand scudded by sea foam. Kim narrowed her eyes, trying to see the distant figure more clearly.

"Oh my God, Joe."

He turned his head. "What?"

"She is gorgeous. You didn't tell me she was beautiful!" Her voice was low, sounding a little shocked.

"I didn't get a good look at her yesterday, only her back."

"Well, you can see her now – see a whole lot of her in that bikini – and she's stunning. Completely stunning."

"Mm-hm," Joe said, trying for a neutral tone.

Kim punched him softly on the back.

"You can look, Joe, I don't mind. Look all you like. As long as it's me you love."

Kim rubbed herself against his butt and smiled when he reached around to rest his hand flat against the back of her waist.

"Always," he said.

Kim dropped her right hand until the fingers rested lightly over the thick bulge in Joe's swim trunks.

"Is this for her, or for me, Joe?" Her fingers cradled the shape of his half-erect cock.

"Who do you think?"

"I'm not so sure. Oh God!" Kim gasped. The woman was closer now and she reached up and tugged casually at the straps on her bikini top, easing them. The movement lifted her breasts, for a moment exposing pale undersides.

Joe's cock filled, and he wondered if the reaction was because of Kim's hand or the sight of the woman. She released the straps, her breasts settling back, heavy inside the bikini top. Her long belly was flat, tapering to a slim waist, flaring only slightly to narrow hips. The bikini bottom didn't match the top, different color and style, light gray where the top was black, cut square across her legs like a pair of jockey shorts, scooped low at the front to exposed a long expanse of skin below her navel. The material, some cross of nylon and lycra, clung to every fold and curve, her pubic mound prominent. The woman had been looking down at the sand, but now she raised her head and they both knew she caught them watching through the window. Joe sensed Kim jump and try to hide behind him. He suppressed a smile. The woman tilted her head, letting them know she was watching them back. She raised her hand in a casual wave. Joe lifted his own, returning the greeting.

"You gonna say hello too, Kim?" he asked.

Kim lifted her hand off his cock and offered a small wave. The woman's teeth flashed, white against her tan, before she turned away from them, back to the closed up house next door.

"I wonder who she is?" Kim returned her hand to Joe's trunks.

Joe shook his head. "No idea. I assume she owns the house or is allowed to use it."

"Wow," Kim said.

"Wow what?"

"Nothing. Just wow."

Joe laughed. "I didn't realize women affected you that way."

"We all have our little secrets, Joe."

"Not from each other," he said. "Never from each other."

Kim's head rested against the back of his shoulder. "No, you're right. Never from each other." Her breasts flattened against him and he felt dampness where her nipples leaked, a small amount of milk soaking two layers of cotton.

"You're not into women, are you?" Joe asked, his curiosity, and his cock, piqued at the thought she might be.

"No… not really. But I guess I could be a little curious…" Kim wrapped her fingers around the ridge of his cock, found him harder than before.

"I didn't know that."

"Well now you do." She lifted her hand, burrowing in past the elastic of his trunks until her fingers found his bare cock.

"Is Ami asleep?" Joe asked as Kim began stroking along his length.

She nodded against his back. "Do you think you want to lie down too, Joe?"

"It might do me good," Joe said.

"Me too," Kim said.

Joe followed his wife upstairs to the bedroom. Kim lay back on the bed and looked up at him with open need in her face. Their sex life was good before Ami was conceived, but during pregnancy Kim went wild, constantly needing sex. Different positions, different ways, different places and times. Joe was more than happy to oblige. Something about the way Kim's body changed as life grew inside her, about the way her stomach bloomed, becoming smooth and tight, turned him on more than he could bear. After Ami was born there came a gap, a hiatus in their normally vibrant sex life as Kim recovered; but she still continued to suck his cock until he filled her mouth. Kim worked hard restoring her figure and four months after Ami's birth she looked even better than before. Because Ami was feeding, Kim's breasts remained large and Joe was constantly turned on by their sensitivity, turned on by the milk leaking from her nipples. He was aware of it now, staining the front of her t-shirt around the hard peaks tenting the loose cotton.

Joe moved to close the blinds covering the bedroom windows, but Kim said, "Leave them, babe."

"What if someone looks in from the beach?"

Kim rolled on her side and stared through the window, shutters forming dark wooden shadows beyond the glass, slicing the beach and sky into strips. "So?" She started touching herself outside her bikini briefs, lifting her leg so Joe could see more clearly where her fingers lay.

"Fuck, Kim." Joe sat on the edge of the bed, his cock painful inside his trunks. "We can't do this." The tall windows in the bedroom reached almost to the floor offering an uninterrupted view of the beach, equally presenting a clear view in for anyone outside. It was the reason the shutters covered them. When closed.

"Mm, we can," Kim said, "I want you to fuck me, Joe, but slow, real slow."

She reached across and tugged at his trunks. They had to come off, and as she pulled them down his cock jerked up hard against his belly and Joe caught Kim watching hungrily, her expression one Joe recognized, knowing its meaning.

"Oh my God, do you think you can manage slow?" she asked.

"I can try, and if I can't manage slow maybe we can carry on anyway."

"Oh, I like the sound of that." Kim grinned and Joe saw her expression change as a new idea came to her. "Okay, fast is good too, Joe. Cover me in cum and afterward we'll do it again but slower."

Kim lifted her hips from the bed as Joe tugged at her bikini briefs, allowing him to draw them down her slim legs. Kim had shaved her pussy for the birth, claiming someone had told her it was more hygienic, although Joe believed she was making the story up. Then a couple of months after the birth she started shaving there again. As the lowering bikini exposed her sex Joe's eyes devoured the smooth exposed skin between her legs. She knew how much he liked her smooth skin; Joe too recognizing being shaved excited Kim too. She wanted him to do the same, but other than allowing her to trim his pubic hair short and shave his ball sac he had resisted so far, although the idea was beginning to grow on him, lodging insidiously in his mind as he wondered what it would be like to fuck her with no hair between them at all.

Joe pulled his t-shirt over his head. Kim lay passive, waiting for him to strip hers off. First he leaned over and kissed the edge of her thigh, his nose touching between her legs, his tongue following and he found her thighs wet, her labia plump with arousal. Kim pushed against his lips and Joe drew back teasingly. She lifted her arms above her head, exposing all of her now taut belly. Joe grinned and slid a hand beneath the cotton and traced a line with his finger around her right breast, deliberately avoiding her nipple until she squirmed and he took pity. The instant his fingers touched the hard nub Kim jerked and gave a muted cry, pushing the back of her hand against her mouth. Joe felt the slickness around Kim's nipple as milk expressed. She didn't seem able to stop the milk since arriving at the beach house, whether because she was producing too much or because of the sex neither of them knew or cared. The break from routine had made them both more sensitive to arousal. They couldn't get enough of each other, and when Kim's breasts leaked it turned Joe on more than he thought possible. At times, they more than leaked. When she was especially aroused at the moment of climax her right nipple, the one Ami used less, would spurt warm milk against him, never failing to tip him over. Just thinking about it was making Joe tremble, and he knew he was incapable of lasting as long as Kim needed to achieve her own satisfaction.

"Is quick okay?" he asked, and she grinned.

"Oh yeah, Joe, as fast as you want babe."

Joe pulled the t-shirt over Kim's head, mussing up her blonde curls. Joe watched Kim slide around on the mattress until her head hung over the edge, knowing exactly what he wanted. She lifted her knees so her heels rested on the far side of the mattress. Joe took his weight on his hands, pressing down into the covers on either side of Kim's hips, and let the aching head of his cock lie against the side of her face.

"No – fast." She reached for him, breath hot against his

belly, hair brushing his thigh. Her fingers found his cock and he groaned as she brought him to her lips. She placed the thick head of his cock against her mouth and waited. Joe trembled against her lips, letting Kim feel his need and when he pressed she offered token resistance, forcing Joe to push the head of his cock between her lips.

Joe arched over Kim, his tongue seeking her pussy as his cock slid deeper into her mouth, curving against her, belly pressing against her nipples and she gasped around his cock even as it filled her mouth. He was deep inside her now and she pushed back against his hips. Joe eased the pressure, aware Kim was at the limit of what she could take, wishing he could bury himself entirely inside her mouth but knowing that was not possible, satisfied with what she offered. They had tried in the past, slowly and quickly, and Kim could only ever manage half his length before starting to gag.

Joe stretched, his tongue finding the slippery wet sensitivity between Kim's legs as she stroked his balls with her nails, making him shiver. His ball sac tightened and he knew he was on a hair trigger and this would take no time at all. As his tongue opened her sex Kim pressed her thighs against his face and pushed up, gaining what pleasure she could before he exploded. His balls stroked against the bridge of her nose and Joe imagined what Kim would see, no longer worried about any part of his body on display to her because she told him nothing was out of bounds, proving it now as her hand searched along the cleft of his ass and a fingertip found his asshole. That simple, single touch was all the trigger he needed.

Joe's mouth lifted from her pussy as the curn filled his cock. He jerked into her mouth, for a moment going too deep before regaining a measure of control. The first hard explosion of semen splashed against Kim's tongue and then he was filling her mouth, his seed slippery and slick on her tongue and he watched as she allowed it to slide from her lips, slide along her upturned face as he erupted again and again until she had no choice but to swallow.

Joe held himself against her, shaking, his cock slowly deflating. Kim sucked hard around his softening length, drawing the last reluctant drops from him and he pulled away and sat on his heels on the bare wooden floor, bent over and kissed her, his face upside down to hers, his tongue exploring her mouth. The taste of his cum in her mouth excited him, and Joe was aware this was turned her on too.

Joe knew Kim was only starting, and the thought of how aroused she had become since arriving at the beach began to thicken his cock again; not hard yet, but longer than a moment before. He tugged her around on the bed, flipping her onto her front, kissed his way along her slim back, kissing the deep valley running along her spine. Slowly he worked his way up, knowing she liked certain things, knowing the places on Kim's body that made her shiver. Here, to the right of her spine, below the shoulder blade – something extremely sensitive lay at that point though neither knew exactly what. The right degree of pressure was required, and Joe pushed two fingers down into the muscle, finding a tiny node, some microscopic point, aware he had found the exact spot when Kim bucked and yelped.

Joe laughed. "Are you *sure* you like me doing that?"

Kim shook her head. "I'm not sure. Yes. No. It hurts, but it's exquisite as well… like there's a direct connection through to my tits." She laughed into the bed covers. "God Joe, I've squirted on the sheets again."

"Don't sweat it." He released the pressure of his fingers and kissed her on the same spot. "Get 'em as wet as you like. We've got plenty more."

"What's the cleaner going to think when she finds a basket full of stained bed sheets?" She half turned on her side, looking back at him, seeing the amusement in his face.

"She'll be jealous, I guess."

"Too right," Kim said. "I still want it slow, Joe, don't forget." He saw her glance down to where his three quarter erect cock swung against her ass, wriggling against him, making him stiffen further.

"Is Ami down for a while?" he asked, nuzzling into her neck, searching for more pleasure points. He had identified three or four around her neck. Kim loved her earlobes being sucked and nipped. Loved when he kissed just behind her ears, when he sucked against her neck, around the side and back.

Kim groaned. "She'll be down for an hour at least. She took a good feed."

Joe kissed her behind one ear, gooseflesh dimpling instantly against her arms and he smiled. His fingers stroked her back, sliding down between the cheeks of her ass and Kim pushed one leg to the side, parting herself in encouragement. Joe laid his finger against her sweet pink asshole and slowly moved the tip in a circle.

"How long can you hold out?" he whispered into her neck.

"Ages," Kim said. "Ages and ages."

"Are you sure?" Joe lifted his finger to his mouth and wet the length against his tongue. When his finger returned to her ass he pressed lightly, opening her. He watched his fingertip work inside Kim's tight asshole, the sight causing his cock to harden fully. Kim must have felt him stiffen and slide against her side because she twisted, not so much that Joe's attention on her ass was distracted, but enough to allow her hand to reach him.

Joe slapped her fingers aside. "No – you come next, babe. You're not allowed to touch."

"Want to touch," Kim groaned.

Joe shook his head. "No. Tell me what else you want."

"You know what I want."

"I do, but you got to tell me. You got to ask me, Kimmy."

"Not fair."

Joe removed his fingertip from her ass, wetted to the knuckle and pressed back inside, further than before. The tight ridged wall closed around his finger and his cock was fully erect now, pressed against Kim's side. She reached for him again. Joe used one hand to grab her wrist and lift it above her head. She tried to reach around with the other and he caught that too, held them in his large hand, easily gripping both wrists, pressing them down on the bed above Kim's head.

"Joe," Kim moaned. "Please babe, you know what I want you to do to me."

"What's that, Kim?" Joe said into her ear, nuzzling a sensitive spot until her arms pimpled again. The cheeks of her ass and thighs as well, blooming into gooseflesh as he nibbled and licked her neck.

"I want you to play with my ass, Joe," Kim said into the pillow, her voice muffled.

"I am, babe," he said, pressing his finger deeper. Kim pushed back against him, trying to force it further inside.

"More," she said. "I want more than your finger."

"What do you want?" he asked, kissing her narrow shoulder blades. He moved lower, tracing the edge of her ribs with his tongue.

"Oh yes Joe, go on babe..." she sighed.

"Tell me," he said again, pausing as his lips reached the first bloom of her ass. His finger turned, pushed, withdrew and entered again.

"Oh please, Joe... please..."

He licked the side of her hip, drew his tongue to the center of her back and kissed once more. Kim lifted herself, opening her ass to him. Joe lifted his head and started to move back along her side, kissing as he went. He felt her trying to free her hands, trying to wriggle from his grasp.

"No!" she gasped. "Other way, Joe, please, the other way."

He smiled against her skin, so smooth and soft, so wonderfully scented by motherhood.

"Tell me," he said.

"You bastard," she hissed.

"You got to tell me what you want, Kimmy. Bad girls only get if they ask."

"You know, Joe. Don't make me say it, babe."

"I don't know, Kim. You got to tell me."

"Ohh..." Kim groaned into the pillow, twisting hard against him and he gripped her wrists tighter and held her down, but he moved his mouth along her back until he reached once more the spot where her spine tucked inside the flare of her ass and she stopped fighting him.

"Ask me, Kim," he said, and something in his voice caused her to shiver.

"Lick me," Kim said.

"Where?" Joe whispered.

"Lick my asshole, Joe."

He grinned, finally moving down, letting his tongue trail saliva along the deep crack of her ass. He hesitated, teasing again before moving to his target. He withdrew his finger, placed the tip of his tongue where his finger had been and circled Kim's perfect pink opening.

"Like this?" he asked.

Joe sensed her head shake somewhere up out of his sight.

"No, Joe. Inside. I want your tongue inside my ass."

Joe stiffened his tongue and pushed, barely opening her, tasting the musk of her ass, loving the way she tasted, loving every single thing about her.

"Like this?" he asked, withdrawing.

Again the shake of her head. "Inside, Joe," she moaned. "All the way inside me."

He grinned and returned to the spot he knew was Kim's most sensitive, repeated the process but this time pushing harder, opening her wide to his tongue and probing inside. The ridged muscle walls granted willing access and he pushed again until his lips pressed flat against her ass, his tongue deep inside. Kim lifted up to him, raising her hips high so he entered as deeply as possible, pushing back against him. Joe finally released her wrists, used his hands to lift her hips against him, and Kim reached underneath, her arm against his face as she pushed her own fingers into her pussy. Joe heard a soft liquid sound as she probed herself, smelled the aroma of her sex coming from between her legs.

This obsession with her ass was something new. Something Kim had wanted since getting pregnant. Almost at once the slightly staid lovemaking they had enjoyed was swept aside. Joe still remembered the almost electric shock that ran through his body the first time she rolled over and stuck her ass in the air, making plain what she needed. He had been tentative that first time, until discovering how wonderful she tasted, and how the act excited him, the taboo arousing them both.

Kim lay beneath him now, close to coming, and he pulled away. She groaned as Joe reached underneath and tugged her fingers from her pussy. She wanted slow, he could give her slow.

He dragged himself up and gripped his cock, placed the head against her wet asshole. They had tried this several times before, both wanting this, but the act proved impossible, Kim too tight. They had persisted as her belly grew but each time, however long they took in preparation, however much lube they applied, when Joe pressed, pushing the thick head of his cock against her ass, Kim encouraged him before crying out as her tight orifice rejected any invasion. It wasn't the pain, she said, she wanted him inside her, but he was too big and she too small. Since that attempt his tongue and finger had been what she wanted, or what she had settled for, still wanting more, always hoping to take the next step.

Joe teased Kim, pressing lightly, watching as her ass widened around the head of his cock.

"Yes," she gasped and he pressed harder, but what they were attempting was impossible. Kim pushed back against him, pushed hard but the physics were wrong, camels and eyes of needles, so instead he humped against her, his cock lightly touching her ass and when her legs began to collapse he pulled away again and gave her a moment. Kim shivered and he saw she was on the point of coming. He stroked her back, the cheeks of her slim ass, slipped his hand inside her thighs and pulled them open.

"Fuck me, Joe," she said.

"I thought you wanted slow?"

"Fuck slow. Do me, babe, do me now."

Kim lifted her hips in the air. She twisted and turned her back to Joe. His cock was solid and aching, pulsing in time to his rapid heartbeat. He grasped her hips and walked on his knees between her legs, let the tip of his cock rest lightly against the engorged lips of her pussy.

For the first time since starting he looked at the north window, his higher position allowing him a view across to the other house. He wondered if the blinds hid them from view or not, and realized he didn't care. The idea of the beautiful stranger seeing them fuck ran like an electric current through his body. He pressed forward and slid inside. Kim gasped once before putting her head down on the edge of the bed and pushing back onto his cock.

Joe reached around and cupped a breast, aroused at the slickness against his palm as Kim leaked milk. He let a small amount gather in his palm before spreading the warm liquid over her breast and Kim moaned into the covers. Joe kissed her shoulder, stroking steadily into her now, hearing her growing excitement, knowing she was almost ready.

When he looked up again the woman had come out on the faded porch and was standing with her arms wrapped around the back of her neck. She had changed into a pair of denim shorts and t-shirt, a gap between shorts and top showing her navel, full breasts stretching the top. She was looking out across the beach toward the sea.

"Don't stop," Kim gasped, and Joe realized he had slowed.

"She'll see us," he said.

Kim lifted her head and saw the woman. Joe paused, waiting for her to turn in their direction.

"Don't stop, Joe," Kim repeated.

He started to thrust once more, expecting Kim to drop her head again, but she kept it raised, continuing to gaze at the woman. Maybe a hundred feet separated their window from the porch of the other house. Not far.

Kim tightened around his cock and Joe recognized the signs. She was within seconds of coming.

The woman lowered her arms, bent at the waist and placed her palms flat on the wooden floor of the porch. She performed the movement easily, naturally, expending no effort. Kim moaned and reached beneath herself, finding Joe's balls with her palm.

The woman straightened and shook her shoulders, stepped down off the porch and turned right, toward their house. Her head stayed down until she reached the corner of the porch. As she turned to go behind the house she lifted her eyes and gazed across the gap. She was staring directly into the bedroom window, directly at them. Her expression didn't change, and Joe was unable to tell if she could see them or not.

"She's watching us fuck," Kim gasped, but didn't stop, if anything riding back harder against Joe, starting to twitch and gasp as her climax gathered and peaked. "Fuck me, Joe," she grunted.

He gripped her hips hard and thrust deep inside.

"No!" Kim gasped as she shook. "On my ass. Come on my ass, Joe."

He pulled out as the first splash of semen erupted from his cock, aimed and let most of his stream splash over Kim's parted ass, and she jerked and cried out as Joe's semen sprayed hot against her. Joe watched his seed slide along the crack of her ass as a second stream erupted, and he aimed the jet directly against Kim's asshole. He looked up, and the woman was still standing beside the house. She had stopped on the corner of the porch, only a hundred feet separating her from their window, and she continued to look across. The idea she was observing them raised conflicting emotions in Joe. Excitement at being watched by her, embarrassment for the same reason. Excitement won and he shot again, arcing harder so the stream of cum spattered along Kim's back. Her head was up and she too was looking across to the other house, mouth open. She bucked suddenly as a second climax hit her and milk splashed from her right breast and pooled on the sheet.

Joe finally moved beyond the oblivion of his climax and leaned over Kim, spreading the slippery semen across the cheeks of her ass, pushing some inside her ass with his finger. Kim sank on to her belly, her head to one side, hair plastered around her face and neck.

"She saw us, Joe," Kim whispered.

"I'm not sure." Joe lay beside her, stroking her back.

"She did. She could see us. She was watching you come on me."

Joe kissed her shoulder. "How do you feel about that, if she was watching?"

Kim giggled. "Made it special, Joe. Made it really special."

Joe looked past Kim's shoulder as the woman turned away, continued walking along the side of the house to where the rusted fender of a pickup showed. He reached around Kim and cupped her breast, wetness under his hand where she had splashed herself, and pulled her back against his body, wanting more of her.

***

Joe tore salad leaves, reached for the small Sabatier from the wooden knife block on the beech worktop, and used it to peel an Avocado. He tossed the soiled knife in the wash-bowl before reaching for the big knife, his favorite because the sleek metal oozed quality and purpose. Joe had always liked quality. Quality was what first attracted him to Kim. The knife sliced the tomatoes without effort, Joe unaware of doing anything. He sliced cucumber as though made of air. He loved this knife, so instead of tossing it after the first he gently washed the ten inch steel blade then dried the metal carefully before slipping the knife back into the slot in the heavy wood block. Behind him he heard Kim snort. He turned to see Ami clasping her breast.

"What?" he asked.

"The way you make love to that knife I'm getting worried about you, Joe."

"It's a work of art."

She made the snort again. "You know what they say about men and knives."

"No, what do they say?"

Kim used her free hand to make an obscene gesture, reminding Joe of what they had been doing only a few hours before.

"Yeah, well, you don't seem to mind a little *knife action* now and then, I've noticed." He jerked his hips at her.

Kim laughed, disturbing Ami who grizzled at her interrupted feeding. Kim took the opportunity to change her to the other nipple.

"You making out you got ten inches as well?" she asked sweetly.

"Never had any complaints," Joe said, grinning.

Kim chuckled and winked at him. "I wonder what that would be like, Joe. A ten inch cock."

"Not sure about ten inches," Joe said. "Four might be more suitable. You'd probably be able to get four inches up your ass."

"Oh, Joe!" Kim threw a cup at him, laughing. Joe reached

out and snatched it from the air one handed, placed the cup on the worktop.

"Only thinking of you, babe," he said.

Chapter 5

After lunch was cleared away Joe stretched, cracking joints in his back, and said, "I'm going stir crazy, Kim. I need to get out and do something. You want to come along the beach?"

Kim shook her head. "I might sunbathe if you don't mind taking Ami with you so I can get a break?"

"Sure," Joe said. "I'd love to take my daughter for a walk. Well a carry, anyway."

While Joe found the baby sling and settled Ami, Kim finished putting plates away. Kim disappeared into the bedroom, returning as Joe stood on the porch trying to decide which direction to go. North would take him past the other beach houses and to where the beach was busier – though not so busy this time of year. If he turned south dunes rose inland and he could walk a mile to where the river cut through to the sea. Ami gurgled against his bare chest, tiny hands waving beneath his chin, trying to reach up to his face. Kim had changed out of t-shirt and shorts into bikini bottoms and a loose, almost transparent throw slung around her waist. She had not bothered with the bikini top, tempting Joe to forget all about his walk and take her straight back inside.

Truth was he did need to get out so he kissed Kim, slapped her on the butt and said, "Don't burn," before striding off across the soft sand.

He walked down to the edge of the breakers where the sand was firmer under his toes and increased his pace, covering the ground quickly. There was a mile to the point, but it was good to have Ami bouncing gently against his chest, arms and legs waving. Her head turned as she gazed around at everything, and Joe wondered what she saw with those brand new eyes. He hadn't been sure about this break – thinking he was going to be away from work for too long, but now he was here and the first week was ending, the tension he carried in his shoulders was fading too; the tension he only became aware of through its absence.

Joe walked along the beach, staying close to the waterline. As he neared the point where the river cut through the dunes he noticed a figure sitting among the sea grass. He thought it was the same woman they had been watching swim, the woman who used, but did not appear to be staying at, the house next door. The woman who may have watched him fuck Kim. Despite this Joe waved, not wanting to appear unfriendly, but whether she didn't see him, or simply didn't want to acknowledge his presence, no return signal was offered.

On his way back Joe slipped Ami from the sling and stood her on the sand, his hands around her small chest, fingers meeting together around her. He walked her to the surf line and watched as she lifted her feet as a wave came in, placed them back when the sand uncovered again. Joe went a little further out and Ami squealed in surprise and delight when foam flecked from a breaker and rolled across her pudgy legs. She lifted them again and laughed, and when the next wave came Joe let the water touch her toes before lifting her high above his head and she squealed even louder. He repeated the motion over and over again, Ami never tiring of the game. Joe hugged her back against his chest and buried his face against the fine hair covering the top of her head, russet blonde like her mother's. He smelled the sweet baby scent of his daughter, smelled the milky aroma. He hugged her against him, filled with love for this tiny creature that he and Kim had created between them.

He was still dipping Ami's toes in the water and throwing her into the air when a voice said, "Hi, you're staying in the Bradley place, aren't you?"

Joe turned to find the mystery woman standing back from the water line. He had been so wrapped up with his daughter he hadn't heard her approach. Despite the warmth of the afternoon she wore faded jeans with a tear in one knee and an old NYU sweatshirt, and she hugged her arms around herself as though cold. Close up Joe was even more enchanted by how lovely she was. From a distance she looked good; close to she was remarkable. Her hair hung back over her shoulders, long, wavy and unruly, pale brown streaked with almost blonde where the sun had bleached it. Her eyes were a sharp gray, dark gray edging into blue.

"I didn't know it was the Bradley place. We call it the beach house."

She laughed. "They're all beach houses."

"I guess," Joe said.

"How old is she?" the woman asked, indicating Ami who was gurgling contentedly as Joe held her against his chest, her legs kicking up and down.

"Six months, and a bit." Joe laughed. "It's funny. After she was born we knew exactly how many days and hours old she was, then we went to weeks, now it's months. I might be able to work out the days and hours but we don't need to anymore. Have you got kids?"

His question was casual, but he caught a shadow passing behind her eyes as she shook her head. "No, no kids."

Joe nodded, not wanting to probe further in what appeared to be a sensitive area. "Do you live around here? I guess you must, I think we've seen you every day since we arrived."

"I live in town on the other side of the island. I come down to clean the houses when folks leave, keep an eye on them if they're empty. I use the Harper's place – next door to you – when they're not staying. They let me change and use their shower."

"You swim every day?" Joe said, more of a statement than a question.

"Every day I can."

"How about in the winter?"

She nodded. "Then too. I've got an old wetsuit I use when the water turns cold. I like swimming."

"Me too," Joe said.

She nodded, standing barefoot on the edge of the waves, in no hurry to move away.

Joe found himself looking down at her left hand and said, "You're married?"

She caught his glance and lifted her hand, turning it to display the narrow gold band, a slight puzzled look on her face as though she was surprised to see it on her finger.

"I'm Joe, by the way," Joe said, and offered his hand, tucking Ami under his other arm where she responded with a loud burp.

The woman laughed and took his hand, her fingers slim and warm inside his. He held the grip for a moment longer than politeness dictated but she made no move to pull away.

"I'm Jenni," she said. "Jenni Adams."

"Pleased to meet you Jenni. This disgusting bundle is Ami, and my wife is Kim."

"Hello Ami," Jenni said, leaning down to stare into the child's bright eyes. Joe was pleased when Jenni didn't put on a childish voice to speak to Ami. He hated when people reverted to gibberish talking to young kids.

Ami gurgled some more and reached her miniature, perfect hand out toward Jenni, who allowed the baby's fingers to close around hers. Ami laughed and gripped Jenni's index finger tight inside her fist.

"She's got you now," Joe laughed. "Once she's got that grip you'll never get away."

"I don't think I want to try," Jenni said, again an undercurrent of sadness in her voice.

"Are you going back?" Joe asked. "Because I think you might have to if she doesn't let go."

"I'm going back," Jenni said. "Do you mind me tagging along?"

"Mind? What's to mind?"

"Well, you don't know anything about me. Folks are funny with their kids around strangers. I understand that."

"Ami's got good judgment," Joe said, smiling down at his daughter, fist still wrapped around Jenni's finger. "Besides, you're not a stranger. We've watched you for a week now."

Color flushed Jenni's cheek and Joe wondered if he had said the wrong thing. He didn't want her to think they had been spying on her, even if that was exactly what they had been doing.

"I've been watching you too," she said. "You three are such a perfect unit..."

"I'm going to walk back," Joe said. "Come with us."

Jenni fell into step beside him, her arm stretched across to allow Ami to continue grasping her finger.

After fifty yards Jenni laughed and said, "Are we going *all* the way back like this?"

It suited Joe. Jenni was forced to walk close if she wanted to keep in contact with Ami, and now and again her leg brushed against his, the unscented smell of her body drifting over him.

"Do you want to carry her?"

Jenni stopped unexpectedly and Joe skidded to a halt, but not soon enough to prevent Jenni's finger slipping from Ami's grasp. Ami's eyes went wide and her bottom lip jutted out.

"Can I?" Jenni asked, her voice almost too quiet to be heard above the soft waves.

Ami had started to sniffle, and Joe knew a crying fit was being worked up, never entirely sure if Ami meant it or whether she had already calculated the best method of getting her own way.

"I think you better had if you don't want to be deafened." He held Ami out toward Jenni.

Ami, sensing the movement, looked up into Jenni's eyes and the sniffle died as a slow smile spread across her face. Joe watched as Jenni's face softened in sympathy and then she was placing her fingers gently around Ami's small body and Joe transferred her across. Ami laughed. Jenni lifted her and laid her against her breasts and Ami laughed again. Joe saw his daughter bury her mouth against the soft mounds beneath the sweatshirt and start trying to burrow in. Jenni watched her squirm, looked at Joe, embarrassed.

"She thinks you're going to feed her," Joe laughed.

"Oh God!" Jenni said. "What do I do?"

"Lift her on your shoulder, unless you want to be dribbled all over. She'll forget about it once she realizes you're not going to feed her."

Jenni lifted Ami to her shoulder, stroking her back as the sniffle returned. Joe, standing slightly behind, put his hands over his face and then pulled them apart and said, "Boo!" Ami laughed, never tiring of the game, and as Jenni started walking again he fell in behind and repeated the move. Jenni looked over her shoulder at him and grinned, strode on, and Joe took the opportunity to admire the way her ass filled her jeans, at the way it moved in miraculous and wonderful ways. He realized he needed to be careful. He would never cheat on Kim, but that didn't mean he wasn't incredibly attracted to this woman. He had to take care and not let slip any hint of those emotions.

Ami was ecstatic on Jenni's shoulder, her eyes starting to close, her head resting against Jenni's neck as her body went loose. Joe speeded up and fell into step beside this vision of a woman.

"So what does your husband do?" Joe asked. "I can't remember, did you tell me his name?"

Jenni shook her head. "No, I didn't. His name's Mark. He's got an auyto-shop in town... most of the time." Her words lacked emotion, and once more Joe sensed something being held back. Jenni looked down at the loose little body snuggled against her shoulder and her face softened. "She's perfect," she whispered. "You are both so lucky."

"We are," Joe agreed.

They walked on for a while, Joe comfortable in Jenni's presence, admitting to himself he was becoming aroused just being close to her.

They had gone a half mile when Jenni asked, "What do you do, Joe? And Kim, does she work?"

"Kim stopped when Ami came along. She's not sure if she's going back. I think we might want a couple more kids first."

"You can afford to do that? So what is it you do?"

Joe hesitated, not sure how much he wanted to let out, how she might take it. Some people became strange when he told them who he was.

Jenni slowed and looked at him. "Oh God, you're not a gangster or something, are you?"

Joe laughed and stopped. "No, nothing like that. Worse. I write. Books. Thrillers."

"I'm impressed." Jenni's eyes widened, but Joe sensed the emotion was forced. He observed the reaction often. "So have I read anything you've written? Do you write under your own name? What is your last name?"

"Fransiscus," Joe said. "Joe Fransiscus. You might have read one of my books." He made an effort to keep his voice casual.

This time the sudden flare in Jenni's pupils was real. "Oh fuck. Oh my God, I'm sorry," and she looked down at Ami, blissfully asleep on her shoulder. "I didn't mean to cuss in front of your daughter," she whispered.

Joe laughed. "It's okay, she's very broad minded."

"You're *the* Joe Fransiscus? The *Dead Reckoning*, the *Dark Waters* Joe Fransiscus?"

Joe nodded.

"No wonder your wife doesn't have to go back to work. Oh my God, Joe." She looked at him, and he was disappointed in her reaction, wondering if he shouldn't have followed his instincts and told her he managed a bank.

"It's only a job," he said.

Jenni laughed, a little nervousness showing. "To you maybe." She looked out over the ocean, looked back and seemed to be making some decision. "Okay. I'll try and pretend it's only a job. I promise I won't ask for your autograph or anything tacky."

Joe laughed, his shoulders relaxing. "Are we going to be friends then?" he asked, discovering he was nervous waiting for her reply.

Jenni looked shy again. "Do you want us to be?"

"I do. I'd like that a lot. Kim too."

She looked up into his eyes and he thought he saw a spark of interest deep inside their steel gray. "I'd like us to be friends, Joe."

They walked on, the atmosphere between them different now, but not uncomfortable.

Another quarter mile went by and then Jenni asked, her voice casual, "So how long are you staying at the house?"

"We're booked for a month," Joe said. "Though we might want to stay longer."

"Fantastic," Jenni said. "You want to come swimming tomorrow?" Her question sounded throw away, as though his reply didn't matter to her one way or another.

"I'd like that," he said.

"Will Kim come as well?"

"Kim hates the water. Hates the ocean. I can't even get her to get on a boat. I wanted us to go on a cruise last year and she refused point blank. We almost didn't come here because she knew she had to come over on the ferry."

"It's only a half mile," Jenni said.

Joe laughed. "I know. But it's not the width that worries her, it's the depth."

Jenni laughed with Joe. "I promise not to raise the subject again then."

Ami started to grizzle and wriggle on her shoulder and Jenni slowed and looked toward Joe, raised her perfectly shaped eyebrows. They had not been plucked or fashioned in any way, just naturally perfect.

"She needs changing, I expect," Joe said.

"Changing? Oh, I see, you mean changing."

Joe laughed. "Here, give her to me and I'll swap her nappy for a clean one." He took the waking infant from Jenni and once more their fingers brushed, the touch electrifying him. "You might want to look the other way, and maybe step back a few paces. This is not always pretty." Joe started pulling baby changing equipment from the rucksack.

"I expect I've seen worse," Jenni said, squatting down beside him, fascinated by the operation.

Joe grasped Ami's ankles in one hand and lifted her, easing the soiled nappy from underneath. Ami lay quiet, content, used to this ritual. He laid her down on a sheet of kitchen towel before using another to wipe her down. Once satisfied Ami was clean he lifted her again and slipped a new nappy under, pulled the velcro tabs tight around her belly, wrapped all the mess up inside the old nappy, folded the edges in and used the tabs to keep everything secure. He repacked the rucksack, putting the dirty nappy package in a side pocket and smiled at his daughter, who was laughing and grabbing at Jenni's long curls as she leaned over her. Jenni played along, swishing her hair to tickle Ami's face and arms. Joe sat back on his heels and observed the two of them, something raw and scary welling up inside him.

"You want to take her again?" he asked, watching the way Jenni played with Ami as though she had been doing this her entire life.

Jenni looked back at him, tanned face beautiful. "Can I? You don't mind?"

Joe laughed. "Mind someone else doing the carrying?"

Jenni lifted Ami gently and cradled her against her shoulder. "She weighs nothing."

Joe laughed again and pushed back to his feet. He offered a hand and Jenni accepted the offer, a natural move making it easier for her to stand. Joe released his grip as soon as she was on her feet. "She's almost twenty pounds now," Joe said.

"She doesn't feel heavy," Jenny said.

They walked on but after a couple of hundred yards Ami began to grizzle again.

Jenni looked down at her. "She hasn't filled her nappy again, has she?"

"She's hungry," Joe said. He looked ahead, the beach house now visible, perhaps a half mile distant. "We might make it back if we're lucky."

Ami had other ideas. She nuzzled against Jenni's breasts, aware only of soft pillowing mounds, knowing this was where dinner came from. Joe glanced across, not sure whether he ought to be looking or not. Ami's mouth knew where nipples should be and she was wetting the front of Jenni's sweatshirt. Jenni smiled indulgently.

"Sorry, honey," she said. "I would if I could, but this well's dry."

"I'd better give her a bottle," Joe said. "Before she dribbles all over you."

Jenni laughed. "I don't mind."

Joe stopped and searched in the rucksack, found a small flask filled with Kim's milk to keep it at body temperature, and a feeding bottle. Joe poured the bottle half full before offering to take Ami.

Jenni cocked her head to one side. "Can I do this too, Joe?"

"You sure you want to?"

She nodded, flushing, and Joe tried to keep his eyes raised and failed. Ami had wetted a large circle around Jenni's nipple, and the suckling had brought it erect. The wet sweatshirt molded around the fullest point of her breast and a puckered nipple showed as though uncovered. Joe passed the bottle and repacked the rucksack. Sitting on his heels he watched as Jenni slipped the teat down against herself, positioning it directly over her breast where Ami's mouth continued to search for satisfaction. Joe experienced a wave of lust rolling through him, making his head swim. He wanted to nuzzle against those breasts instead of Ami. How would it be to taste the sea on her body?

Ami found the teat and latched on it hungrily and Jenni kept her cradled to her breast, as if feeding the infant. The tranquility and pleasure in her eyes was unmistakable. Ami sucked at the bottle, gulping noisily, taking in as much air as milk.

"Don't let her take too much or she's likely to throw everything straight back up all over you," Joe said.

Jenni slipped the teat from Ami's grasping mouth and a tiny cry emerged.

"A little at a time," Joe said, watching as Jenni allowed the teat back, waited, withdrew, returned it, the motion so erotic Joe stiffened inside his trunks, unsure if he was capable of standing now even if he wanted. He couldn't take his eyes of this woman feeding his daughter with such contentment in her eyes. He followed the curve along her side to her hip, narrow but obvious, jutting at the waistband of her jeans. He scanned down over slim legs, back to take in the way the denim snugged tightly between her thighs, sure he could discern the outline of her full pussy, the faintest hint of an opening where the jeans pulled tight. Her waistband was low at the front, her sweatshirt rucked up where Ami wriggled and sucked at the bottle cradled to Jenni's breast, and a band of tanned skin showed, the dimpled lower edge of her navel, and Joe realized he was making the situation worse for himself and turned his head, looking beyond the two of them at the breakers.

Before too long Jenni said, "I think she's finished." She

held the empty bottle out to Joe. Ami nuzzled gently against Jenni, satisfied. Joe took the bottle, again their fingers touching, the contact throwing a jolt along his arm and he wondered if she sensed the same thing too, or only him.

"You'd better put her on your shoulder," Joe said. "Here, put this over you." He stood, aware that if Jenni glanced down the evidence of his arousal would be obvious; not quite as prominent as a moment before, but unmistakable. Why would she do that, Joe asked himself? He was the one losing his composure around here. He shook a small white towel and placed it over Jenni's shoulder. His finger brushed against the skin of her neck where her sweatshirt had slipped aside, but she seemed unaware of the touch, and he let his finger linger a moment longer than he should.

Jenni lifted Ami to her shoulder and Joe pulled his hand away. "Do I pat her back or something? Is that how you do it?"

Joe laughed. "Rub gently, in a circle. She's going to burp, but if you're gentle she won't bring too much up. It helps if you walk as well. I think the movement eases the wind."

Jenni started to move slowly, walking as though on hot coals, each bare foot lifting and stepping like a gazelle. Joe put the empty bottle back in the rucksack, stayed where he was for a moment, kneeling, watching Jenni's ass flex and move as she took those tiny steps. Ami let out a giant burp and Jenni laughed. She glanced back and almost caught Joe's eyes practically devouring her.

"Am I soaking, Joe?" she asked, her eyes sparking.

He joined in with her laugh and stood, slinging the rucksack over his shoulder and walking to join her. "So far so good. Let's get her back. She'll probably sleep for a while now. Do you want to come in and meet Kim?"

Jenni glanced at him. "I'd like that. What will she think about you bringing strange women home?"

"You're not strange," Joe said.

"How can you be sure? For all you know I might be a crazed islander intent on stealing pretty children."

"In that case next time Ami starts crying at three in the morning I'll give you a call. You'll be welcome to take her then."

Jenni gave the little bundle sleeping on her shoulder a hug. "Don't tempt me," she said, her voice so soft Joe barely heard, but he did hear the emotion.

"Besides, you're not a stranger," Joe said. "We've watched you swim every day." As soon as the words left his mouth Joe realized how perverted they might sound and his pace slowed.

Jenni laughed. "You think I didn't know you were watching me?" she said, her voice low, and Joe tried to work out what he could hear. Acceptance, encouragement, disappointment, disapproval?

"What I meant to say was Kim would love to say hello. You will come in, won't you?"

"If you're sure, Joe?" Jenni asked.

"I'm sure," he said, nodding firmly, the moment filled with unspoken expectation, but Joe feared it might just be on his part.

***

Jenni let him walk ahead a little, watching the way his slim ass moved inside the baggy swim shorts, cradling his baby against her shoulder, enjoying the way Ami's legs pressed against her, enjoying the way Ami seemed to take to her, unafraid and trusting. Jenni didn't know much about kids, would like to know a lot more, but Mark had made it clear he didn't want to bring any brats into the world. According to Mark the world was fucked up enough without another wailing mouth to feed. Jenni had tried working on him, which was always tough because Mark didn't listen much to what she said, and when he did listen gave even less attention to her words. Jenni accepted she would never be a mother. Almost twenty-nine, a prime time of life for children if it was going to happen, time left too but she felt the clock ticking and didn't see Mark changing his mind.

Twenty-nine, she thought. Time for a change, maybe. Time to do something about her situation instead of pretending she didn't care, instead of pretending things might get better. Nothing was going to get better, she knew, unless she did something herself to make it better.

Ahead of her Joe kicked at an empty shell, leaned over to

pick a piece of wood up and she watched as his shorts pulled snug, cupping his ball sac between his thighs and she flushed, shivering with sudden lust. She hadn't felt this way, this out of control, since Paul. Jenni wasn't sure if she wanted this or not. Wasn't sure if she needed this, not now, not ever, then thinking suddenly – if not now, when? She had to make the decision she had been putting off for far too long. Had to decide what she wanted from her life. More of the same or something else? But what else… and how far did she want to go?

Chapter 6

As they approached the beach house Joe saw Kim stretched out on the sun lounger. She had carried the lounger off the porch, set it up on the dry sand in front of the house, angled directly toward the sun. She was lying on her front, wearing only tiny black bikini bottoms.

"Hey Kim," Joe called as they walked up from the tideline. "We got company. You want to get some clothes on, babe?"

"Don't worry about me," Jenni said. "I'm all grown up. I'm sure I can cope with a little nudity."

Sounds good to me, Joe thought, but he said, "Kim's a bit of a slut when it comes to flashing herself around, Jenni. I wouldn't want you to get the wrong idea."

"Why not?"

Joe looked at her, but she was grinning and he realized she was teasing.

Kim stirred and Joe wondered if she had been asleep. She liked to sleep in the afternoons now, since they had arrived at the beach, often taking herself to bed, alone if need be, for a nap after lunch. Kim rolled on to her back, scrabbling for her bikini top and cupping it around her breasts. The top was miniscule and her sleep fuddled movement left one nipple peeking free. Joe reached down and slipped his finger inside and tucked her away, her nipple responding instantly to his touch, and Kim smiled sleepily.

"This is Jenni," Joe said. "She was kind enough to carry Ami most of the way back."

Kim held her hand out and Joe pulled her to her feet. Kim kept coming, wanting a kiss, and Joe brushed her lips, feeling a little awkward in front of Jenni. Kim's lips curved into a smile under his and Joe grew nervous.

"She's such a sweetheart," Jenni said, slipping Ami off her shoulder and turning her around to let Kim take her.

"Not at three in the—"

"We've done that," Joe said, laughing, and the two women joined in.

"Nice to meet you at last," Jenni said. "I've seen you around since you moved in, and nearly came over to say Hi, but I thought you might want some privacy."

"You'll stay for coffee, won't you?" Kim asked, then before giving Jenni chance to answer said, "Put some on Joe, we're going to talk about you behind your back." Kim handed Ami to Joe. "Put her down before you start the coffee."

As soon as Joe took Ami, Kim slipped her arm through Jenni's as though they had been lifelong friends and leaned across and whispered in her ear. Jenni's face flushed briefly and her eyes glanced at Joe, and he wondered what the hell Kim had said.

"Go on," Kim said. "Coffee. I need strong coffee. Have you been for your swim today?" The last aimed at Jenni.

Joe took Ami upstairs to the small back room next to their bedroom and laid her in the cot, carefully turning her on one side. Ami was gone to the world, her mouth suckling on her thumb, tiny legs twitching as she dreamed of the coming day when she might walk on her own, without Joe's strong hands to support her. Joe stood at the side of the crib, lost for a while in the wonder of his daughter, then sighed and went down to the kitchen to start coffee. He watched Kim and Jenni outside, sitting at the bleached wooden table on the wide porch, heads together, talking animatedly. What was Kim plotting now?

When the coffee was brewed Joe loaded a tray with mugs, sugar, cream and the coffee pot, shook a pile of chocolate cookies on a plate and carried everything outside. Kim had pulled her dark blue cover-up around her, the move only serving to accentuate the sex appeal of her body, which showed clearly through the gauzy material.

"Are you not swimming today?" Kim asked, offering a tiny pout and Joe wondered what she was up to now.

"I walked instead," Jenni said. "I need to get home soon. Mark gets back at six and he likes his dinner on the table." Joe watched the cloud settle behind her eyes again as she talked about home.

"Tomorrow?" Kim said, ignoring the sudden change in mood. "You're swimming tomorrow?"

"Maybe. Tomorrow's Saturday, change-over day. I need to clean the empty houses and get them ready for new tenants. I'll try, if I get time. If you want me to." She looked at them both, looking up from eyes shyly downcast and Joe was once more knocked out by her beauty and he wondered if she was aware of how she looked. She didn't give the impression she was, which only made her even more alluring.

"How many changes have you got tomorrow? You can't do all these houses, surely," Kim said.

Jenni laughed, her mood lightening as the conversation forced her to draw her back from that gray place she had drifted into. She added cream and sugar to her coffee and sipped. "This is good. I take care of the six houses this end. I prepared your place before you moved in. I left you clean linen last week, on the porch."

"I wondered where that came from," Kim said. Joe was thinking about the state they had left some of the bed sheets in, wondered what Jenni thought of the milk and cum stained sheets, found no shame in his heart nor guilt in his head.

"So how many changeovers tomorrow?" Joe asked. "We're a bit out of season now, aren't we? Will we be getting new neighbors?"

"In the Harper place? No, not next week. The week after I think a family's coming down, but they're in the Parker house which is right at the far end. I've only got two places to clean and make up. I'll bring your linen and take the old stuff away." She stared into Joe's eyes, passing a message back. Yes, I have seen what you have done, but it's okay. We're all grown-ups here and know what goes on behind closed bedroom doors. "This really is great coffee, Joe. How did you manage to land a catch like him, Kim, rich *and* obedient."

"Lies and blackmail. And of course I f-"

"Kim did no such thing," Joe interrupted. "She's an editor. Was an editor. No, *is* an editor," he laughed. "She worked on my first book. We spent a lot of time together, and I fell in love."

"Only you?" Kim asked, raising her eyebrow.

"*We* fell in love. Sorry, babe, *we* fell in love."

Kim stuck her bottom lip out and Jenni laughed. "God, a normal family. Wonderful."

Normal? Joe thought. Are these thoughts in my head normal? Is the growing obsession I have about you, about your body, is this normal, with my gorgeous wife sitting across the table from me?

"Try and come over," Kim said. "Ami likes you, and I'm simply desperate for some female company. Are we going to be friends, Jenni?" Kim leaned over the table and took Jenni's hands inside her own, stared into her eyes with the question hanging in the air.

Jenni flushed and her eyes sought escape by staring at the distant breakers, their sound faint as the breeze came off the cooling land, bringing the hot scent of sun baked earth. The day was moving toward dusk.

"I hope so," Jenni said, so quietly they barely heard.

Kim laughed, sitting back. "Yes, we will. The three of us." She looked brazenly at Joe, passing a message he would ask her about later. Jenni glanced at him as well, her steel-dark eyes bright with a message of her own, one he thought he understood but needed to be sure about. He would definitely need to talk to Kim.

"I really am going to have to go." Jenni finished her coffee and stood. "I'll bring your linen over last, after I've finished the other houses, and if you've got time we'll go for that swim."

"Not me." Kim raised her hands. "You and Joe can swim. He'll enjoy the company. I don't like to think of him swimming all on his own, and he loves it so much."

"I don't mind," Joe said, and then realizing how that might sound added, "But I'd love to have your company, Jenni."

"Oh, get a room, why don't you," Kim said, and after the flare of shock in Jenni's face flushed bright beneath her tan she burst into laughter.

"I did warn you about Kim," Joe said.

"You did?" Kim asked. "What exactly did you warn her

about, Joe?"

"Your honesty, my darling," Joe said.

"I should think so."

"Hey, guys, I do have to go. Thanks for the coffee, and letting me steal your daughter for an hour. I'll see you tomorrow if I can." Jenni stood on the top step of the porch, hesitating.

Kim rose and went across and hugged her, kissed her softly on the side of her face. She turned back to Joe and raised her eyebrows. Jenni was just starting to turn away and Joe rose and went over and hugged her as well, a little awkward because she was on a step lower than him and her head barely came to his chest. She lifted her face and he brushed her cheek with his lips and caught the scent of her as he had before, salt and sun oil and something deeper and more animal underlying everything else.

***

Kim went inside, and when Joe found her she was standing on the upstairs balcony watching Jenni cross to the other house. Joe stood behind Kim as Jenni climbed into the cab of the old pickup. The engine started noisily, clattering until settling after a moment. Jenni's arm waved through the window as she drove off. Kim's fingers reached across for Joe's and found his hand. They stood unmoving until the truck crested the rise in the road that ran back between the dunes, and Jenni must have been aware they were still looking, because her arm came out through the window again and then she was gone.

"I like her," Kim said.

"Me too."

"I know *you* do. You were practically salivating watching her."

"Was not!" Joe turned to go inside but Kim stopped him, slipping her arms around from behind, pulling him back against her.

"It's okay, Joe. You can let your eyes pop all you want. Mine were doing the same. She's some piece of work, isn't she?"

Joe found himself nodding, heard Kim chuckle.

"I might even let you fuck her," Kim said, her face pressed

flat against his strong back.

"Very kind of you, I'm sure."

"No, I mean it. I wouldn't mind, not at all."

"Kim?" Joe turned inside her arms and slipped his own down around her waist. "Where's this coming from, babe?"

Kim shook her head. "Nowhere. I have no idea, Joe, I really have no idea," and she lay her head against his chest, sobbing.

"Hey, babe, what's wrong?"

Kim shook her head and pulled from his arms and turned away, leaning against the balcony railing, the blue cover-up billowing in the wind, Kim's hair tugging around her face. Tears continued to streak her cheeks and Joe held her again, Kim tensing, only slowly relaxing against him as he continued to hug her.

"Tell me," he whispered into her ear.

"I don't know. Hormones, I guess. I'm just so fucking horny all the time these days, Joe, so fucking horny. I was looking at Jenni and wondering what it would be like to have my tongue between her legs, what it would be like to suck on those big titties of hers... God, Joe, am I disgusting you?"

Arousing me, he thought, his cock stiffening quickly, aware Kim would feel it too as he pressed the bulge between the cheeks of her ass.

"Joe?"

"Mm?" He nuzzled into her neck, gooseflesh speckling her arms.

"Am I awful for thinking these things?"

"Nothing you think or do is awful, babe. Nothing at all."

"But I'm not normal," she said.

"Good. Normal is dull."

"I'll try and behave myself, Joe, I promise."

"Don't try, babe," he said, reaching under the cover-up and finding the knot of her bikini behind her neck. He tugged, letting her breasts tumble free, cupped his palms over them and Kim pushed back against him.

"Make me come, Joe, please?" Kim said, a harsh need in her voice he hadn't heard before. She leaned against the pale wooden railing of the balcony and stepped back, setting her feet apart. Joe went to his knees and tugged at her bikini briefs, pulling them to her knees. The scent of her pussy enveloped him, and when he lifted his hand and pressed a finger between her legs, as soon as he parted her tight opening juices gushed out wetting his hand.

He kissed the back of her thighs. Kim lifted one leg and placed her foot on the bottom rail running across the balcony six inches above the boards, pushed back against him. Joe licked up along the crack of her ass but he knew she didn't want that. He lifted her against his mouth, arching his neck back so his tongue and lips were against her pussy. He kissed her labia, tasting the copious juice that flowed from her, reached with his tongue and flickered against her clitoris which was hard, ready.

Kim pressed against him, her breath ragged, her head hanging over the porch. Despite the thickening air anyone passing along the beach now would be granted a full view, but neither cared or even thought about what they were doing so publically.

"Make me come, Joe. I need to come so badly."

He pushed three fingers inside her, not gently, opening her wide while his tongue flickered and joined them. Kim came fast when she needed to, and Joe knew this was one of those times. She was rocking back against his tongue, each movement accompanied by an animal grunt, and before he was ready, wanting to tease her longer, Kim cried out, her voice sounding across the empty sand, so loud gulls rose and wheeled away from the breaker line as she gushed against his mouth, squirting on his tongue and he lapped her, swallowing the delicious fluid she offered, aroused now beyond restraint. Kim's knees buckled and he rose and gripped her waist, holding her up. He fumbled with one hand, tugging his trunks down and his cock slapped out against Kim's ass and she grunted.

Joe pushed his leg between hers, dipped and Kim reached back seeking his cock, helping guide him to her. She leaned over further and Joe pushed hard into her pussy, lifting her feet off the ground. He gripped her hips, holding her off the floor as he pounded hard into her from behind.

"Uhn–uhn–uhn." Kim grunted with each thrust, touching her breasts with one hand, holding herself against the railing with the other. "Imagine I'm Jenni, Joe. Imagine you're fucking Jenni like this. Imagine how tight her pussy is around your cock, this big, thick cock, imagine her big tits bouncing and swaying. She'll have long hard nipples, Joe, and a wonderful ass. Imagine I'm... uhn... I'm watching you fuck her... Imagine... oh shit... imagine I want to watch you fuck her... Oh God Joe, I'm gonna come again!"

So was Joe, so fast and strong he was unable to control himself. He slapped Kim on the ass, something he had never done before, and she yelped and shook beneath him. A violent jet poured from his cock as though his entire body was emptying inside her. Kim felt the force of his climax too, and it triggered another deep inside her. Joe pulled her against him, trying to force his cock beyond any place he had reached before, emptying again and again and again.

He gasped, pulling away, his cock sensitive beyond bearing and Kim dropped to the floor, spun around and took him instantly into her mouth as he deflated, drawing the entire flaccid length of him onto her tongue and pressing her lips hard against his pubic hair. She rocked her face against him, her hands cupping his ass, pulling him tight against her lips. Kim held his cock in her mouth until Joe felt himself twitch and harden. Only then did she release him, sitting back before climbing up his body and allowing him to taste his cock on her mouth.

"Where the hell did that come from?" Joe gasped, breathing hard.

Kim shook her head. "No idea. Wherever it was we need to find the place again, Joe. My God, I've never come like that before. Twice times in as many minutes!"

"What are we going to do?" Joe kissed her hair.

"What we've always done, babe. Fuck each other's brains out."

"I love you so, so much," Joe said.

"I know. And I love you even more. More than anything in the world."

Joe laughed. "Except Ami," he said, and Kim giggled, recovered now.

"Of course except Ami; that goes without saying."

Joe knew he and Kim were one thing, and the other was Ami. He recalled the shock of emotion which filled him the instant he first laid eyes on his tiny daughter, bloodied and bedraggled and a little blue in the face, and the wave of love bursting inside him was something only a parent could experience. His love for Kim was constant and deep, but his love for Ami was visceral and raw and he knew the emotion all fathers experienced, that he would protect her with his own life if necessary. He knew Kim felt the same; perhaps, if possible, even more so because she had carried this jewel of life inside her own body for nine months.

Chapter 7

Jenni put Mark's plate in front of him. Cheap steak, fries, no vegetables because he refused to eat them. A beer sat open near to hand and he sipped from the can before picking up his knife. He cut his steak into chunks, put his knife down and used the fork in his right hand to spear meat, a fry, more meat.

Jenni sat across from him, her own plate holding a different meal. She had grilled half a snapper, boiled potatoes from the garden, added salad from the same small plot. Growing anything with the sea all around was difficult, but she persevered, rewarded when she ate her own produce. The corn would be ready soon and she loved it coated with butter. She would need to eat that when Mark was out because he said watching her disgusted him the way she attacked it, butter dripping down her chin.

"There's one house still open on the beach," Jenni said, trying to draw him into conversation.

"Mm-hm."

"Young couple from away. They got a baby. Six months old."

Mark stopped chewing and looked across the table at her until she averted her eyes, only once she was concentrating on her own plate did he pick his fork up again.

"I don't know how you can eat that crap."

"I like it."

"Fuckin' rabbit food. No wonder you're so skinny. Need a bit of meat on you."

Jenni looked up, something sparking inside. "Would you like me more if I put weight on, Mark? If I was bigger?"

He snorted. "Can't turn shit into gold."

Jenni had no idea why he treated her this way, putting her down constantly, making out she was ugly. It caused her to doubt what the reflection in the mirror showed, made her doubt her own judgment. She ate the rest of her food in silence, all taste gone so she chewed without being aware of the clean sweet sea tang of the snapper. She was trying hard not to let tears flow, trying not to let him catch a glimpse of how much he hurt her.

It hadn't always been this way. Jenni loved him once. Thought she loved him. Now she couldn't remember if the emotion was love or something else. She had been escaping her reputation, escaping her wild past. Nineteen, a year out of high school but the wildness had started long before then, the word out about her. Jenni no knickers. Blow job Jen. Want a good time, want to get laid? Hey, try Jenni, she'll fuck anyone. What made the whole thing worse was that everything they said was true; in those days she would fuck anyone, try anything. Not because she was easy, but because she loved sex, loved how she felt as another body moved against hers. She became frustrated, trying to find satisfaction somewhere but ending up giving satisfaction only to others.

The winter after she turned nineteen she made herself a promise to stop sleeping around, to find someone who loved her, who didn't want her because she had a great ass and big tits and would let them fuck her any which way. That promise led her to choose Mark.

He hadn't chased after Jenni, instead it had been the other way round. Mark was quiet, two years older than Jenni, a steady job working for his Dad's auto repair shop and he looked okay; not great, but okay. He didn't want to fuck her every second of the day and night. That had seemed a blessing. If only she had realized what it meant, but instead she welcomed the respite, welcomed the lessening of the rumors. When she and Mark married a year later it was like a comfort blanket wrapping around her.

At the start life had been okay. Acceptable, anyway. She grew used to the fact he didn't want sex as often as she did, learned to live with that. She grew used to his moods and the comments, always denigrating her, always making out she was nothing special until she doubted all the things anyone said to her that made her believe differently. Things had changed so slowly Jenni couldn't pin down any exact moment when she started to hate the marriage and what she had become. Like a toad in a pan of water, not aware it was growing hotter until too late, she accepted more and more degradation. Sometimes the contrast between what was then and what was now stopped her cold and she wondered how things had managed to get so bad.

Jenni started looking around for satisfaction elsewhere only when she could stand the frustration no longer. Always with visitors, always with strangers until Paul, never with anyone from the island. She had been discreet. Mark might not want her, but she believed if he discovered what she did in secret he might kill her. Sometimes she wondered if that would be a better solution. Let him find out; kill or cure, literally.

Jenni cleared the plates and Mark went to the hallway and pulled on his coat.

"Are you going out again?" she asked, instantly aware it was the wrong question tonight when he whirled back, strode across the kitchen and slapped her across the cheek.

"Why? D'you care?" he snarled, turning away. "Don't bother waiting up."

The door slammed and Jenni ran water into the sink, allowed her tears to run free across her cheeks and drop to mix with the hot water. Through the window the evening lay dark on the hillside behind their small house, made even darker by heavy cloud. In the distance she heard thunder, saw an occasional far off stab of lightning glowing through cloud.

Maybe she'd get lucky and one of those bolts would seek ground through Mark, when he finally made his way back from the bar. She went upstairs and searched through the small bookcase in the spare bedroom. Somewhere, she knew, she had copies of both Joe's books and she wanted to read them again. She found the first, a battered hardback she had bought from a thrift store. She took the book downstairs and curled up on a chair and opened it to the back cover where a photograph showed Joe. He looked younger, his hair shorter. He looked sexy as all hell. She turned to the front page and started reading.

***

Joe and Kim took Ami out in her sling, walked the dark beach, pale phosphorescent waves rolling in, the sound soft in the night. The moon had risen three-quarter full and stars filled the sky other than to the east where high thunderclouds gathered. Wind blew in intermittent gusts, and from far over the sea came a faint, distant sound of thunder. The smell of seaweed gathered above the tideline offered its half-unpleasant scent to the air, and they walked close to the surf where the wind blew in over the ocean

"Storm coming," Joe said.

"Ayuh," Kim said and they both laughed. She had been raised in New England, but no-one would guess unless she wanted them to.

When they came back into the house they tucked Ami, still sleeping, into her cot then lay under a single sheet, listening as the wind gathered strength and worried around the house. The waves sounded louder and thunder came more frequently. Neither of them wanted to sleep, but they didn't want sex either so they lay side by side, chastely holding hands, listening as wind spattered the first raindrops against the open bedroom window.

"The rain's going to come in," Joe said. "I should get up and close the window."

"Leave it. Nothing's going to spoil."

They fell silent again. Rain came more persistently and the room cooled. Kim rolled over and hugged herself against Joe, her hand cradling his balls.

"Joe?"

Thunder rolled and he waited for the sound to fade. "Mm-hm?"

"I wasn't joking before."

"About what?"

"There's something about that woman, Joe. I've never been turned on by anyone except you. Why is that?"

"She doesn't know how incredible she is, does she."

"Mm... We've joked about this before, Joe, but I'm not joking now." Kim's fingers were stroking his balls, and even though he didn't want sex his cock responded.

"Tell me what you want, Kim," Joe said, the subject of their conversation exciting him.

"We're going to kill each other if we don't stop." Kim rolled on top of him, slid down so his cock entered her. She lay flat against him, hardly moving, her lips against his shoulder. Joe felt her nipples harden against his chest, her breasts flatten.

"You know I love you," Joe said.

Kim chuckled. "I want to... I want to fuck her, Joe," she said, and it was out in the open, her voice sounding a little shocked.

"Me too, babe, me too."

"You do?"

This time Joe laughed. "You're kidding, aren't you?"

"A little, yeah. You don't mind I want to fuck another woman?"

"I guess I'm supposed to."

"You are. So what would you do if I fucked her?"

"Do you want me to mind?"

"I need to know, Joe. I can't tell you what to feel."

"Is it what *you* want, Kim. Do you really want to fuck her?"

Kim was moving against him now, slowly, softly, but she was tight around his cock and he knew she was going to make him come eventually, make him come like she always managed whether he was in the mood or not, he was so crazy in love with her she was capable of making him do anything she wanted.

"I think I do."

"It's not just some... I don't know, some infatuation? You've never shown interest in women before."

"I've never told you, Joe."

"You have?"

She wriggled. "You still haven't answered my question. How would you feel about it if I fucked Jenni?"

"Depends."

"Depends on what?" Kim's voice had grown soft and despite his cock lying rigid inside her pussy he felt her body loosen against him.

"If I can fuck her too."

Kim's mouth formed a smile against his shoulder. "As well as, or together? I think I like the idea of all that."

Joe laughed softly. "Who are we kidding? She's probably not interested." Joe grasped Kim's ass in his hands, encouraging her to move a little faster but she teased, responding by going completely slack on top of him. Her passivity aroused him even more and he felt his cock harden painfully inside her.

"Oh, she's interested," Kim said. "A girl can tell these things. So can you. Trust your instincts. She's interested, Joe." Kim's voice was soft, slurred, her body loose as she lay against him. Her bones were melting, muscle dissolving.

"Do you want to fuck right now?" Joe asked. He was rigid inside her, encased inside the slick warmth of her pussy.

"No, not really. But it's nice like this." Kim squirmed against him.

Joe stroked her back as she loosened further. Thunder sounded close to, and Kim jerked as it brought her awake but almost instantly Joe felt her drift again. Her mouth opened where it lay against his shoulder and saliva dribbled on to his chest. She began to snore softly against his skin and Joe smiled into the dark and let his hand rest in the small of her back. He was still hard but knew any chance of real sex was gone. That was fine, because this was good too, so comfortable with Kim sleeping on top of him, her body molded against his. Every now and then she mumbled and her hips moved, as though she dreamt of what they might be doing.

The storm came in full force. Rain lashed the windows and Joe heard it spatter on the floor, but Kim was right, nothing would spoil. Thunder crashed overhead and Kim stirred again. Joe took the opportunity to ease her body off his. His cock slid from inside her, cooled as air caressed it, and he rolled Kim on her side and spooned around her, his cock lying stiff along the crack of her ass, his hand wrapped around to cup her breast and eventually sleep claimed him as well.

**

Mark woke Jenni as he returned home, late and drunk, stumbling around the bedroom while he let his clothes fall wherever he managed to get out of them. He fell into bed beside her in his shorts and reached across without a word. This was how they had sex now, as though he needed to get himself drunk enough to want her.

Jenni tried to ignore him, tried to feign sleep, but Mark didn't care whether she was conscious or not. Jenni turned her head aside as he climbed onto her, not even bothering to pull his shorts down. He fumbled his cock through the elastic of his shorts and pushed her legs apart. She was dry, but it hardly mattered because his cock was slim and he forced himself into her, humping rapidly, coming fast and rolling away.

He fell asleep in moments, and when she was sure Mark was comatose Jenni slipped from their bed and went along the hall to the bathroom, washed the evidence of his anger away. Anger it was, she knew. There was no love in what Mark did to her.

Jenni had gone on the pill after the episode with Paul, not wanting to take any chances, knowing Mark would go wild if she fell pregnant. Truthfully, she did not want Mark's child now. A child, yes, but not his. Jenni was also honest enough to admit to herself that the pill was an acknowledgment she was going to repeat the betrayal of her marriage. The act of taking the small daily pill permission to herself.

She sat on the edge of the bath, hearing the storm batter around the house and made a resolution. She would leave him, if that was possible. As soon as the thought came she felt better, smiling into the mirror, smiling at the pretty woman sitting across from her that couldn't be her because Mark kept telling her she was ugly, so someone else must have crept into the house and taken her place. Good. Maybe it meant she could sneak out without being missed.

Chapter 8

"**Mark, get out of bed or you're going to be** late for work!" Jenni shouted up the stairs. She could have added: *Again*.

Lately Mark seemed not to care whether he his job was there or not. He might work for himself, but the few customers who still came to him would soon drift away if he was never there when they called. Well, if *he* didn't care, Jenni did. They had little enough money coming in, and what Mark earned he drank half of. If not for the cleaning and laundry Jenni did they wouldn't have food on the table. Mark still expected food on his table. *His* table; according to Mark *everything* was his stuff, nothing hers.

Jenni returned to the kitchen and cracked two eggs in the pan she had fried bacon. The eggs spat and crackled, bubbling around the yolk the way Mark liked them. Jenni preferred her eggs soft; she had no idea how Mark could eat them like this, burned beyond all taste, but she knew if she tried to change things she'd earn a slap, or worse.

She turned the eggs over, slid them on a plate next to the bacon, started a new pan for pancakes. Still no sign of Mark. She slid the pan off the heat and shouted upstairs again. No answer. She made her way up. He might not care his job, but she did!

Jenni found him lying in bed. Jacking off. She stood in the door and he grinned at her, unabashed, frantically rubbing his small cock.

"Want some, sweetheart?" Mark's voice shook with the effort of his movement.

Jenni turned on her heel and stamped down the stairs. How dare he! If he wanted sex why didn't he ask her? She had never said no, would *never* say no. Sex was one of the pleasures she treasured, one of the aspects of her life she recalled in memory rather than reality. Good sex, anyway. Who the hell was he thinking about, on his own, in their bed? Not her, for damn sure.

She put the pan back on the stove and cooked three pancakes the way he liked them.

Why am I doing this? The thought ran like fire through Jenni's head. Mark was upstairs jacking off and she stood down here making him breakfast, same as she did every morning. Is this what *he* did while she fried bacon?

Well fuck him, she thought, and tipped the contents of the pan into the garbage. He can make his own breakfast. Pulling on her jacket Jenni left the house, grabbing Joe's book from the hall stand, slamming the door hard, making sure Mark knew she was gone.

Jenni knew she was going to pay for this minor act of rebellion later. Mark would come in drunk and pick a fight, any excuse or no excuse at all, take it as reason enough to start knocking her around. She jumped in her beat up truck and waited while the engine turned over, sounding as it always did as though it wasn't going to start. But it always did – eventually. She drove through town and beyond, toward to the beach. Getting an early start on the cleaning might give her time to see Joe and Kim for lunch. Just the thought brought warmth to her belly where a moment before had been cold anger.

***

It was a little after one as Joe watched Jenni walk from the house next door. Joe and Kim had gone into town earlier, returned with bags of groceries, holding off preparing lunch, hoping Jenni would arrive. Her pickup was parked in its usual place, so they knew she was around somewhere.

Joe heard her knock on the porch side and Jenni dropped a checked bag containing clean linen on the boards. Another identical bag with the old sheets and towels was already waiting for her to take away, Joe thinking again about what might run through Jenni's mind as she washed them, seeing the stains his semen had left on the sheets, the dampness from Kim, the soured smell of breast milk that flowed too copiously.

Joe leaned against the porch rail as Kim came out and kissed Jenni. Kim stood back and looked Jenni openly up and down.

"Looking good, girl," Kim said, and Jenni blushed. It was obvious she had made an effort, crisp cotton shorts to her knees, white linen blouse unbuttoned half way to display the same black bikini top that seemed the only one she possessed, her skin tanned, glowing against the white linen.

"You look good too." Joe saw Kim simper a little, because she knew she did. Joe thought she was being deliberately decadent, wearing the gauzy blue cover-up from the day before, tied above breasts unencumbered by any other covering. The flimsy polyester hid nothing, Kim's breasts on clear display and her dark nipples obvious. She had told Joe she was going to wear nothing at all under the cover-up, but relented when he said that was probably too much too soon, so a pair of tiny white bikini briefs covered her... just.

"We haven't eaten yet if you want to join us," Kim said. "Or are you and Joe going swimming first?"

"I don't know. What do you think, Joe?"

"I don't think he can wait," Kim answered for him. "He's been like a puppy all morning."

"Have not."

Kim gave him a glance that said she didn't believe him, and Jenni laughed. "Are you two always like this?"

"Oh no," Kim said. "Sometimes I tease him a little."

"Let's get out of here," Joe said, and as he brushed past Jenni lifted his hand and let it trail against her shoulder. "If you're ready, that is."

"Sure. Let me get these off." Jenni unbuttoned the rest of her top, folded it neatly and placed it on the bleached table. She unzipped her shorts and let them drop, bent from the waist in the same way Joe had seen yesterday, flexible and unstrained, picked the shorts off the floor and folded them next to her top. She turned and joined Joe, magnificent in her beauty, body gleaming and glowing, hair falling in russet curls over her shoulders. She put her hand beneath its weight and drew it all over one shoulder, a habit Joe had seen her do more than once as they walked back along the beach.

"Enjoy yourselves," Kim said. "Lunch when you get back.

Don't be more than an hour."

Joe waved his hand without looking back and broke into a jog, pleased when Jenni matched him. He glanced across, drawn to the sight of her breasts rising and falling with each stride. The bikini top was tiny, its black cotton stretched tight over her large breasts, the straps cutting lines in her shoulder as the weight of them fell on each step. Joe tried to hold back so he could study the way her ass moved in the non-matching gray briefs but Jenni looked back at him and grinned.

"Eyes front, soldier."

Joe blushed. He increased his pace and passed her easily, heard her laugh and then his feet were in the surf, the waves big after the storm, the sky still scudded with cloud but the air was warm and the sea felt good against his legs. As soon as the water was deep enough he dove in, the tug of a breaker passing over him, surfaced and shook water from his eyes, his too long hair flicking drops around him.

He pulled himself out through the breakers until the water calmed. The waves still came in as big as ever, but out here they were no more than a steady rise and fall, lifting his body, dropping him back into each trough. Jenni stroked toward him with an easy crawl, hair streaking along her back, face lifting to one side as she breathed.

She reached him and trod water, three feet between them.

"I like to swim way out, Joe."

"How far?" He looked into her eyes.

"Way out. I like going too far." She stared back, a faint smile playing on her kissable lips. Joe wanted to drift across and pull her against him, wasn't sure if he did she would offer any resistance. He shivered involuntarily and shook his head, making out he was clearing spray from his face.

"Me too. Is it going to be a race?"

Jenni shook her head. "I don't think so, do you? We can take as long as we like." This time there was no mistaking the intention behind her words. She twisted into a crawl and deliberately brushed past him. As she touched him she turned on her side, as though rolling with the stroke, but the movement brought her firm breast sliding along his flank, her hip followed and finally the silky length of her thigh.

Joe rolled and followed close behind, tempted to reach out and grab her ankle, pull her back against him. Some faint remnant of reserve prevented him. He drifted to one side, trying to keep a distance between them, trying to reduce the temptation.

The ocean cooled as they stroked further from land. Jenni swam well, her movements economic, perfect body sliding through the water as though this medium belonged to her. Joe kept pace, almost equally at home, but he made a splash where Jenni parted the water, he needed to exert more effort, but because he was stronger he was faster than Jenni and after a while he put his head down and pulled ahead.

When he stopped, breathing hard, he looked back and found the shore was now a half mile distant. The swell carried his body with it, remorseless, not caring about such meager beings as he and Jenni.

A strong current plucked at Joe's feet and when Jenni reached him he said, "Is there an undertow out here?"

"A little." He was glad to see Jenni breathing almost as hard as him. "It's fine right now, but can get bad when the tide turns. Don't worry, we'll be back by then."

"I didn't even think about the tide. When does it turn?"

"Couple of hours yet." The swell and current caused Jenni to drift away, and she casually reached across and placed her hand on his shoulder to maintain her position. Joe's concentration centered on her touch, the curl of her fingers across his skin. "The water's cold this far out."

"Are you okay?" Joe asked.

"Fine." Jenni nodded. "I didn't mean I wanted to go in. I like the cold – it make me feel alive." The swell rose, pushing her toward him. Her breasts touched his chest. Then the sea dragged her back and her fingers tightened on his shoulder to stop herself drifting away. "How about you? Do you swim in the ocean much? I don't even know if you can where you come from."

Joe laughed as the current drew her back to him and her nipples dimpled against his skin (only the cold, he thought, making them that rigid), and this time her leg brushed his, brushed between his thigh as though an accident and Joe knew she had felt how his cock was thick inside his trunks. She was drifting again and this time he put his hand on her arm, high up near the top, as though helping her stay close.

"I swim in the ocean when I get the chance, but we're from New York, and the Hudson's not so good for swimming. The ocean near us is as cold as a witch's tit. But we've got a pool at home so I swim every day."

"You look like a swimmer." The water brought Jenni back to him, her belly against his, her breasts flattening on his chest and her other hand touching his waist, holding them together.

"What does a swimmer look like?" Joe asked. His cock ached, Joe afraid it would slip from the leg of his trunks, didn't know if that would be good or bad.

"Slim, muscular, not all beefed up. Good."

"I guess you look even better than that," Joe said.

Jenni smiled. "Why Joe, was that a compliment?"

"Sure."

"So sweet," Jenni said, and this time when the swell brought her against him she grinned and kissed his cheek. "Thank you, Joe, but I know damn well I'm not a quarter as beautiful as Kim."

Joe looked at her, his hand on her waist, Jenni's on his, and the swell tried to pull them apart but they held each other close, fighting the current. Joe had stopped fighting himself.

"You may not realize it, but you are." Joe said. "You're..." he hesitated, giving her a chance to shake her head. Her belly was pressed against his, her flesh cold to the touch. Her thigh brushed against the bulge in his trunks and she moved gently as though the current was doing it, and maybe it was.

"I know what I am, Joe." She was so close he was tempted to lean across the space and kiss her full lips. She would let him, he knew she would let him, maybe wanted him to. What was she thinking? What did she really want?

"I mean it. You need to know, Jenni. Both Kim and I think you might be the most beautiful woman we've ever seen; and we've seen some very beautiful women."

Their bodies were now pressed tight, almost all pretense gone. Joe's fingers wrapped around Jenni's waist, splayed down against the delicious bloom of her ass.

"Get away," she said, breaking the spell by splashing water in his face. "If I didn't know better I'd think you were trying to get into my panties. I'm a married woman, I'll have you know."

Joe knew his mouth hung open. Jenni flipped away on her back, her breasts breaking surface like the back of a diving whale, her belly following smoothly and then her hips, her pubic mound clearly outlined cupped in her briefs and she scissored her legs, opening them wide in front of him so that the plump lips of her pussy showed. She kicked, splashing him again as she moved away.

Jenni rolled on her front and stroked away parallel to the beach. Joe followed, pulling harder to come alongside but still maintained a distance between them. They swam until his muscles ached, finally heading inshore.

As they walked up the wet sand Jenni bumped against his hip and Joe noted she was a couple of inches taller than Kim. She put her hand on his arm, stopping him. Jenni raised up on her toes and allowed her lips to lbrush against his. She dropped back and strode away without a word.

"What was that for?" Joe asked.

She looked over her shoulder, the erotic potential in that one glance almost too much for him. "Just thanks, Joe. For swimming with me. Are we going to do it again?"

He nodded. "Every day, I hope."

She grinned. "Only every day?" The pretense was falling away. Joe sensed Jenni knew exactly what was happening and was a willing, an eager participant.

"Whenever and as often as you want, Jenni."

***

The table in the kitchen was decorated with a cloth and laid with plates, glasses and cutlery. Enticing aromas filled the room. Kim showed Jenni the small downstairs shower, laughing as she realized Jenni knew perfectly well how the house was laid out. Kim brought a robe into the steamed bathroom and left it over the linen basket, risked a quick glance at the other women naked in the shower stall. Kim knew she wanted Jenni, wanted her badly.

When Jenni came out Kim was sitting with Joe at the table, had pulled her cover-up aside to feed Ami, the infant happily suckling on her nipple. The other breast was also free to the air, the nipple hard in sympathy, a narrow trail of milk running down the curve of her breast to form a line on her belly.

Jenni sat across from her and Joe, hair wet and skin glowing, wearing only the robe Kim had left for her, an almost deliberate provocation. Kim caught Jenni staring at her breasts, at the feeding infant and the line of milk.

Kim laughed and speared a lettuce leaf with her fork. "Don't look away. Look all you like, I don't mind."

Jenni flushed, forcing her eyes to rise and meet Kim's. "It doesn't seem polite, does it?"

"I don't mind, honestly I don't. I think it's worse when people pretend not to notice, pretend it isn't happening.

Jenni's gaze dropped again just as Kim pulled Ami from her left breast and transferred her to the right. Milk continued to flow from her nipple as Ami latched on the other breast and Kim knew Jenni was watching it roll down her skin. The feeling of being observed ran through her, making her nipples harden in a different way, then ran down through her belly to spark warmth between her legs. She wanted this woman, in the same way she knew Joe wanted her. She had played with the idea of another woman for a long time, mildly aroused at the idea of what they might do with each other, but this was something different, an obsession now, lodged in her mind and heart. She had to have Jenni. Joe too, she accepted, but she wanted Jenni first. She wanted Jenni together with Joe, she and Joe and Jenni. She played scenarios through her head as her husband sat beside her eating lunch and Ami suckled her and Jenni pretended to eat but was really looking at Kim's breasts.

Kim stared back, watching how the white toweling robe gaped at the front to expose the curve of Jenni's breast, more arousing because of the change of tone, deep tan suddenly cut across where her bikini top had shaded her skin, the main weight of her breast white. Jenni leaned forward, unconscious perhaps of the way the neckline displayed her and Kim saw the weight of her breasts shift, so much larger than her own, and she wanted to suck on them, not in the way Ami suckled on her, but something rawer, something wilder.

Ami's feeding eased and Kim looked down as her perfect daughter's eyelids drooped and closed. She smiled and pulled gently until Ami's mouth unlatched from the nipple, enjoying the rush of cool air against tender flesh. She lifted Ami to her shoulder, not bothering to cover herself, because this was how they were, this was what they did, not needing to cover their bodies in front of each other, and even though there was a new person across the table she was not going to change the way she did anything. She circled Ami's back with her hand until rewarded with a comically loud burp, waited and received a second release of wind. Ami was a limp rag now and Kim handed her across to Joe who took her without a word and carried her upstairs to her cot.

Kim sat back and stared openly at Jenni. The other woman flushed, caught out, her thoughts transparent.

"How does that feel? Feeding Ami?"

"Wonderful."

"Does it make you sore?"

Kim shook her head. "Tender. Sensitive. Not sore, not really."

Jenni stared at Kim's breasts. Kim made no move to cover herself, aware her nipples grew stiff beneath the other woman's gaze. When Jenni finally lifted her eyes Kim stared back openly, trying to answer a question that had not been asked, not out loud.

"Come here." Kim patted the chair Joe had vacated.

Jenni looked at her. She hesitated, then rose and came round the table, sat and allowed her gaze to focus on the trails of milk running down Kim's breasts.

"You can touch, if you want," Kim said.

"What?" Jenni's eyes shifted rapidly away. "What do you mean?"

"You look like you want to touch my nipples. You can, it's

okay if you want to."

Jenni shook her head, long hair drying now and falling back into natural curls that Kim was jealous of. "I wondered... what it would be like." Jenni's voice was barely audible.

"Try." Kim's voice sounded hoarse in her own ears.

The flush on Jenni's tanned cheeks deepened. "I can't."

"I want you to." The hoarseness grew in Kim's voice, wetness pooling between her legs. She pushed her chair back and sat on the edge of the table facing Jenni, placed a hand beneath each breast and lifted, gasping as the movement forced the sensitive tips outward. The shape of her nipples had changed over the months of feeding Ami. They had always stood proud, but now the dark nipples peaked on a plump bed of areole which had filled more as her breasts changed, becoming puffy and large so that her breasts rose in multiple layers to their most sensitive peak.

Jenni's hand lifted, rising toward them, stopped and withdrew. "I can't."

"I want you to touch me." Kim leaned forward, offering herself.

Jenni's eyes locked on her nipples, observing as they stiffened, hardening even more than they already were. Kim reached down and took Jenni's hand, placed it against her breast, allowed Jenni's fingertip to lightly brush against the nipple. The feeling was unbelievable, better than all her imagining.

"Please." Kim leaned further toward Jenni.

Jenni appeared mesmerized as she moved closer, edging toward Kim's perfect up-tilted breasts. Her lips parted and Kim shivered as the other woman's breath brushed warm against her nipple. She released Jenni's hand to slide her own behind Jenni's head, burying her fingers in the thick auburn curls.

"Please," Kim repeated, releasing an indrawn cry as Jenni's lips closed over her nipple. Jenni's tongue flicked out and tapped the stiff nub. Kim saw a trail of her milk on Jenni's tongue and shivered. "You have to suck them. Suck them hard if you want my milk. You do want my milk, don't you?"

Jenni nodded, unable to resist. Her lips closed over Kim's

nipple again, this time closing tightly, the suction building, soft and gentle, not like the demanding vacuum Ami made. This was different, not serving the same purpose. Kim's breasts released their bounty and she felt Jenni draw milk into her mouth. She drew Jenni's wide mouth hard against her and allowed her head to drop back. The sensation was electric, running through her body, making her fingertips and toes tingle. Kim had no idea how far things might have gone if Joe had not returned. She saw him over Jenni's shoulder, standing in the doorway, and wondered how long he had been there. The lessening of pressure on the back of Jenni's head alerted her to some change and she pulled off Kim's nipple, saw her looking over her head and turned.

She jerked upright, flushing with embarrassment at being found out, but Joe's smile was so forgiving her guilt appeared to instantly drain away.

"It looked like you were enjoying yourself," Joe said. "Both of you."

"I was only..." Jenni started, but it was obvious to all of them no excuse was going to work in this situation, not with a line of Kim's milk still trailing from the corner of her mouth.

"Go on." Joe walked across. Kim watched him touch Jenni's shoulder, slipping his fingers beneath the toweling robe so they rested against her skin, urging Jenni back to her breast. "I want to watch you do that again."

Jenni made a noise deep inside her throat, half objection and half need. Kim felt Jenni's body vibrating against hers, knowing exactly what was happening, exactly what she wanted. She had never felt this way before, this raging need, not just for Jenni but for Joe as well, and Kim believed Jenni was experiencing the same raw passion, that she was theirs completely, to do with as they wished. Kim knew Jenni wanted this as badly as they did.

Joe lowered his head and rested his cheek against Kim's left breast, applied gentle pressure and Jenni acceded to his will, her mouth latching back over Kim's nipple. Kim stiffened at Joe's touch, smiled. He turned his head, still keeping his eyes on Jenni, and placed his mouth over the other nipple.

Kim jerked and a tiny yelp escaped her lips, the sensation of both sensitive nipples being drawn on almost too much. She was trembling hard, close to climaxing. Joe's hand snaked inside her thigh, pushing her bikini briefs aside and dipping inside her. She was melting, juices trailing down her thighs, soaking Joe's fingers. She bit hard on her lip, knowing this was going too far, not yet ready to take the next inevitable step. She grabbed Joe's long hair in her fingers and pulled his head aside, shook her head and as he looked up at her she mouthed the word, "No!"

He understood. Thank God, he understood. He sat back and took the chair on the other side of the table where Jenni had been.

Kim wrapped her fingers in Jenni's thick hair and drew her gently away. She came reluctantly, breast milk trailing down her chin, and looked up at Kim.

"You have to leave me some for Ami, sweetheart," Kim said softly.

Jenni sat back, reaching behind to finding her chair, composure ruffled. "Sorry. I was... getting carried away."

"I know." Kim leaned down, lifted Jenni's face and kissed her lips, tasting her own milk, the sweetness flooding her mouth. She kissed Jenni deeply, allowing the moment to draw out, pulled back. "Soon," she said, staring into the other woman's eyes, and Jenni nodded, recognizing the message being sent.

It seemed to Kim as though she was melting; she had never experienced such a welling of lust, burning hot in her belly, spreading to her extremities. She wanted Jenni to bury her face against her breasts again, wanted to kiss her neck and stomach and lovely mouth. She wanted Joe's hard body to be pounding against her, and she believed this would come to pass, if she was patient. She should show some restraint, but could find none. If they wanted her now she was theirs, here in full view of the beach, she would let them take her any way they wanted, completely theirs.

Jenni took a deep breath and sat back and Kim mirrored the move. The mood shimmered and broke, falling away.

"Food's going cold," Joe said, and everyone laughed.

***

Joe and Kim walked Jenni across to her pickup. As she opened the door she saw the copy of Joe's book she was reading still on the seat and reached across for it. Nervous all of a sudden she turned and held it out to him. "I feel stupid, but would you sign this for me, Joe?"

He looked down and laughed. "Sure." He took the book from her. "I haven't got a pen."

"Shit." Jenni leaned back into the cab, searching for something to write with. She found a ballpoint in the side pocket, scribbled on her palm to check it still worked and handed it to him.

Joe opened the front cover, looked sideways in thought then wrote something inside. He closed the book and handed it back to her. Jenni was too nervous to open it in front of him to see what he had written.

"Thanks, Joe."

"Anytime. Before we leave give me your address and I'll send you a copy of the new book."

Jenni felt herself flush. She nodded and climbed into the cab, knowing Joe and Kim were both watching her ass and not caring – no, wrong, caring, caring a great deal. A thrill coursed through her to know their eyes were on her.

All the time driving back to her house on the far side of town, all the while she lugged the dirty laundry into the lean-to on the side of the house, Jenni thought about what was happening to her, wondering if she could go through with this thing, ideas of what could be burning hot in her brain.

She laughed. Of course she would, much too self-aware to know any other outcome was possible. It would not be the first time she had taken relief outside of marriage, and she experienced no guilt for that. Other opportunities had arisen, and although she did not take all of them, some temptations she was unable to resist. Perhaps if Mark had been more attentive, better looking, smelled less or was around a little more temptation would have been easier to resist.

It was not as if she fucked around all the time, and never

with anyone in town. Only occasionally, when something sweet offered itself she was happy to succumb, to take satisfaction for herself.

The first time had been three years after her marriage to Mark, when it was more than obvious how things were going to be. Paul had been the last, but before him there were others. An older married man had attracted her strongly and she had succumbed in the back of his Lexus while she was supposedly helping him unload shopping. Two brothers, nineteen and twenty, older than their age, experienced, who had taken her together one night, lying out on the dunes, their hard bodies moon splashed and remorseless.

Once, almost, another woman, a young wife much like Kim who spent her days sunbathing while her husband wandered the beach watching other women. Jenni had wanted to succumb to her attraction, stopped not by reluctance to make love to another woman but because the husband was never away long enough. Jenni had seen a need in the woman's eyes, knew she wanted Jenni as much as Jenni wanted her. Vacations are short, summer's end, and Jenni chalked that one up on the nearly side of the blackboard.

There were men in town who wanted her, but she was reluctant to journey along that road. Despite the corrosion of any love she might ever have felt for Mark, he was still her husband, and in Jenni's family that meant something. Or had, until the last few years. When Mark starting hitting her she began to consider whether divorce was not a better solution. Even then she didn't see how that could work. Where would she go? Her parents had moved south, tired of the cold winters, and lived in Florida now. She had a brother but he was on the west coast. All she had was Mark and her house and the few friends Mark allowed, and those were not real friends, not the kind of people she could go to for help if things turned bad. The town, this island, was too small a place, and Jenni lacked the courage to leave and start out on her own some place new.

The island defined her, owned her and trapped her.

Until now, perhaps.

Inside her own kitchen Jenni started preparing dinner

before remembering the book. She went out to the pickup and brought it inside, opened the front cover and read what Joe had written there.

For Jenni – the most beautiful mermaid in the ocean
All my love XXX
Joe Fransiscus

His signature was scrawled, indecipherable. It wasn't the signature that caused her eyes to prick with sudden tears, but the lines above. She held the book hard against her breast, as if the book was the man.

Jenni put the book down and returned to preparing Mark's evening meal. He arrived at six, same as he did almost every evening, never working overtime, never stopping on the way home. He sat at the table without washing his hands, ate his food in silence. A cold knot formed in Jenni's gut. Mark's moods were well known to her, and she hoped he would pull out of this one.

Half way through the meal Mark went to the fridge for a second beer, caught sight of the book on the worktop and picked it up. Jenni's blood chilled in her veins. She prayed Mark would lose interest and replace the book, a knot twisting in the pit of her stomach as he started to flick through the pages. He looked at the picture inside the back cover, went to put the book down, setting it on the edge of the worktop awkwardly and it fell to the floor. Mark left the book. He would never pick up anything as useless as a book, Jenni knew, but the way the book fell had opened the front page and Mark stopped as he saw the words scrawled there.

He bent down and retrieved the book, read the words slowly. Mark read everything slowly. He glanced at Jenni, back to the book and read the signature again.

"What the fuck is this?"

This is going to be bad, Jenni thought.

"I told you about the couple in the Bradley place. Turns out he's a writer."

Mark studied the book, turning it over gingerly as though he held something rotten.

"I can see that. What's this crap he's written here?"

Jenni couldn't pretend the words were meant for someone else. "A joke, Mark," she said. "Only a joke. He thought he was being funny."

"Funny? With my wife?" Mark returned to the table, placed the book flat and started eating again. Jenni watched him, waiting, wondering if she might get away this time.

Mark cut meat and chewed, his eyes on the book the whole time. He reached across and opened the cover again, scanned the words, then he lifted the book and threw it hard across the table. It hit Jenni on the cheek, heavy and sharp cornered and she cried out. Mark rose and followed, grabbed her arm and dragged her off the chair so she sprawled on the kitchen floor. He stood over her, hands loose beside him, fingers held straight and stiff along his thighs.

"Pick it up."

Jenni retrieved the book, climbed to her feet.

"Out back. Now." Mark gripped her wrist, his fingers hard, dragged her out the back door into the small yard that had no fence but gave directly onto the sheep-grazed grass that ran up to the spine of the island.

"Burn it!" Mark's voice was cold.

Jenni shook her head, holding the book tight against herself. Mark's fist lashed out and struck her ear. Jenni dropped to her knees, head ringing.

"I said fucking burn it!"

"No!" Jenni screamed at him, getting to her feet again.

"What?"

"No, I won't burn it. This is mine. No-one's ever signed a book for me before."

Mark reached out and Jenni turned away. He punched her hard, low down on the back, twisted her round and grabbed the book. Jenni fought, trying to keep hold but Mark's left hand slapped her face and her fingers came loose. Mark stepped away, his hands tearing pages loose. Jenni cried out and lunged for him again and he hit her casually back handed and continued on. An old oil drum stood on a patch of scorched grass where they burned rubbish. Mark fumbled in his overalls and pulled out a disposable lighter, flicked a flame from it and held it to the pages he had torn out. The paper caught rapidly, flaring up, and he dropped them in the incinerator, tore more free and added them. He turned to Jenni, holding the book open, showing her the front page Joe had signed, ripped it slowly away from the spine, his movement deliberate. Mark held Joe's words over the flames until they caught. He tossed the remains of the book into the drum. Then he turned and started toward Jenni.

Chapter 9

Jenni did not return to the beach house until Friday, waiting for the worst of the bruising to fade. Kim and Joe were clearing lunch from the bleached table on the porch when Jenni came up in her mismatched top and bikini briefs. Kim slipped her arm around Jenni's waist and kissed her on the mouth.

"Joe's nearly ready. We missed you. Where were you?"

"Stuff." Jenni shrugged

"You're okay to stay today?"

Jenni nodded. "Mark's out with his buds tonight. Bowling, again."

Something in Jenni's voice made Kim turn to her. "What's wrong, honey?"

Jenni shook her head. "Nothing's wrong." But even as she spoke her voice caught and broke. Kim reached out and drew her into a hug.

"Tell me, Jen, tell me what's wrong."

Jenni shook her head. "I can't. Nothing. Nothing's wrong."

"There is. Tell me. Is it Mark?"

Jenni sobbed, her head nodding into Kim's shoulder. "He burned Joe's book, Kim. He found what Joe had written and he burned the book. He can't stand seeing me happy, Kim, he can't stand it."

"I'll get Joe sign another one."

"I haven't got another one."

"We have," Kim said. "And if there's anything we can do to help you only need to ask."

Jenni gasped a sob and shook her head. "Nothing. Shit happens, that's all."

"Shit shouldn't happen."

"It does to me. Not you and Joe, no, I can believe that, but to the likes of me shit happens all the time. All the fucking time."

Kim pulled back and looked at the face of the most beautiful women she had ever known, saw the shadows under her eyes, then the dark stain on her cheek.

"He hit you!"

Jenni shook her head, not negation, just a postponement of the truth.

"That bastard hit you!" Kim repeated.

"You don't understand." Jenni made an effort to pull herself together, straightening up, wiping the back of her hand across her eyes. "This is my life. This is what I understand, Kim. Not everyone can be like you and Joe. This is *real* life, and in real life husbands knock their wives about."

"Not the real life I know," Kim said. "You can leave him."

Jenni gasped a laugh. "Yeah. On this island? Where would I go that would be any better?"

"You could-" Kim cut herself off. She had almost said *You can come and stay with us*, but that would sound weird, too much, too soon. Maybe too much *ever*. So instead she said, "You can stay then, if he's out with the guys. Can't you?"

Jenni nodded. "I guess."

"No," Kim said. "You can stay. We'd both love you to stay. Ami would love it. I think she has a new hero figure."

"She's so sweet," Jenni said.

"So you will stay?"

"I guess, if I'm invited," Jenni said, and Kim grinned. Something different was happening today, she sensed it, anticipation vibrating through her body like a drawn bowstring.

Joe came out in speedos, tighter and more revealing than the shorts he had worn the last time, and Kim saw Jenni's gaze drop to his trunks. The curve of Joe's cock was obvious, tucked to one side, a thick ridge pushing against the dark orange lycra. Jenni lifted her eyes and caught Kim watching her and her cheeks flushed.

Oblivious, Joe brushed past Jenni. "Come on, lazybones." He lengthened his stride into a slow jog. Jenni glanced again at Kim before turning to run after him. Kim watched her go, enjoying the way Jenni's ass moved in the tight bikini briefs. She leaned against the porch railing and continued to gaze after them, not concerned when Jenni caught up with Joe and punched him on the side and he reached back and grabbed her around the waist. This thing was going to happen. Kim knew Joe well enough to trust him. She was not going to lose Joe to this woman, however beautiful she was. She knew this deep in her heart, even though they had never before entertained the fantasy they were now playing out.

The couple reached the breaker line and splashed around, kicking water at each other before striding out through the waves, lifting their arms as each breaker rolled in, splashing foam and spray around their lean bodies. The water had reached their waists when Kim saw Jenni stop abruptly and dart violently sideways. Joe turned to her, trying to grab her arm but as she fell backward Jenni knocked his hand aside and leapt away from him. Joe tried to close the gap but Jenni was shouting something, her voice loud enough for Kim to catch the edge of her words even back on the porch, caught her words but not the meaning. Joe stopped and Kim saw him come toward shore, wading as fast as possible. He came back twenty feet, turned and moved across the waves before turning back toward Jenni. She was floating on her back, arms out, hair spread around, tugged and tangled by the waves. Joe grabbed Jenni under her arms and pulled her back to the shore.

Kim ran down the beach, her feet flying over the sand toward them. She reached the shore as Joe was dragging Jenni from the water. She lay back in his arms, face contorted with pain, her left leg held up as though she was trying to push it away from her.

"What happened. What's wrong?" Kim helped Joe with Jenni, not sure what to do and Joe shook his head and put his arms under Jenni and lifted her easily, walked up the beach with her.

"Jellyfish," he said. "Big one. Stung her on the leg."

"Vinegar," Jenni said between gritted teeth. "It's not a bad one, but fuck it hurts!"

"Go ahead," Joe said to Kim. "Find some vinegar. Anything else?" he asked Jenni but she was not listening.

Kim ran to the house, grateful Ami had gone to sleep after

lunch. She found a pint bottle of vinegar, took it out to the porch while Joe carried Jenni the rest of the way. He sat her on the step and knelt beside her leg. The perfect skin was mottled and red all along the front of her thigh, above and below the knee. When Kim leaned close she saw minute stingers hooked into Jenni's skin. Joe took the bottle of vinegar from Kim and tipped it up, letting a little splash against Jenni's leg. She winced and gritted her teeth, but when Joe stopped Jenni said, "No, more. And I'll need some help to shave my leg."

The incongruity of what Jenni said made Kim giggle nervously. "They're pretty smooth already, babe. Shouldn't we worry about these stingers first?"

Jenni shook her head, the pain seeming to recede a little as the vinegar discouraged the nematocysts from releasing their toxin. "More vinegar, Joe. The shaving will remove the stingers without release any more poison. I need one of you to help me do it." She looked at them and they both nodded, and at that moment she didn't care if they both helped. Her leg was a flame of agony.

Joe splashed more vinegar on her leg and Jenni waved her hand. "Enough. Keep some for later. Help me inside."

Joe took most of her weight and she hopped beside him into the kitchen, through to the small downstairs shower room. Jenni sat on the white plastic seat in the shower and held her leg out. The pain seemed to be easing a little, and she laughed harshly. "This isn't how I was thinking we might share the shower, but needs must."

Kim knelt beside Joe, holding a can of shaving cream and a safety razor.

"Lots of foam," Jenni gasped, and Kim let the nozzle spray white foam all over the affected area. Joe ran the razor over Jenni's leg. Kim took the shower head and turned it on but Jenni shook her head. "Not yet. Fresh water will make it worse. Let Joe remove the stingers first."

Kim dropped the shower head and sat on her heels, her hand touching Jenni's hip in a gesture of sympathy.

"Again?" Joe asked. He had removed all the foam, and when Jenni nodded he sprayed again and repeated the operation.

"Okay, more vinegar," Jenni said. The color had returned to her face, and already Kim could see the irritation reducing. Joe poured the remaining vinegar across her smooth skin and Jenni sighed deeply. She looked to Kim and nodded. "You can wash it off now. If you've got some soap and shampoo that'll help neutralize the venom. I was going to ask if you had any baby oil, but of course you have."

"I'll get it," Joe said, moving away.

Kim turned the spray on and poured shampoo on Jenni's leg, working it in with her fingers, trying not to press too hard. Jenni leaned over and added her own hand.

"How do you feel now?" Kim asked, looking up at Jenni's face.

"Lucky. If that had been a man-of-war I'd be on my way to the emergency room. It was only a moon-jelly, thank God. Have you got anything I can take for the pain?"

"Some Tylenol?"

Jenni nodded. "Sounds good. Two."

Kim went to find them as Joe returned and started applying the clear baby oil to Jenni's leg. When Kim returned Jenni had stopped trembling. Kim could see that the slick oil under Joe's hand against Jenni's smooth skin was starting to turn him on. She felt it too and tried to push the arousal to one side. Now was not the time.

"I think I can walk now, but I'm going to need to lie down for a couple of hours." Jenni pulled a face. "I'm sorry guys, this is not what I was hoping for this afternoon."

Kim gave her a hug as Joe helped Jenni to her feet. "It's you that matters, babe. Use our room upstairs, it'll be quieter for you."

Jenni used Joe as a crutch to climb the stairs. Kim followed, amused to see how his cock had filled and now pushed against his speedos. Under other circumstances the sight would be turning her on as well, but at the moment she was content to observe only.

Upstairs Jenni dropped to the bed and sighed. Kim handed her a glass of water and two tablets. Jenni swallowed them, looked down at herself and pulled a face, grabbed Joe's arm so she could stand.

"I'm getting your bed all wet. Kim, help me out of these things. Joe, you'd better find something else to do."

Joe looked at her, his face a comical mask, and Jenni gave a little smile.

When they were alone Jenni hopped around and said over her shoulder, "Unclip me, Kim."

Kim pulled the catch on the bikini top and Jenni let it drop from her breasts to the floor.

"I don't know how we can do this without scraping my leg." Jenni hopped back around, her breasts bouncing enticingly as she moved.

Kim went to her knees in front of Jenni and slipped her fingers into the waistband of the bikini bottoms.

"I'll try and pull these down. See if you can sit when your butt's clear and I'll do what I can to keep them away from your leg."

"I'm so glad you and Joe were here."

Kim smiled. "Anything for you, babe."

"Even this? Isn't this a bit too much like changing Ami?"

Kim looked up along Jenni's perfect body, at the large breasts hanging self-supported, swaying slightly as she breathed.

"I don't think so," Kim said, and Jenni's cheeks flushed.

Kim started working the bikini bottoms down over Jenni's hips. This was meant to be a job, but anticipation thrummed in her chest as the other woman's pubic hair appeared. Darker than her own honey blonde bush would be if she allowed it to grow, Jenni's pubic hair was fine and curled, completely untrimmed but not a thick mat, enchanting Kim. As the bikini came down it caught for a moment where it was pressed into the slit between Jenni's legs and Kim tugged harder, her eyes lingering as it pulled free. She was rewarded with an even better view as Jenni sat back on the bed and lifted her right leg to withdraw from one side of the briefs. The movement opened her thighs. Kim saw a perfect pink slit cradled by plump labia. Kim concentrated, stretching material hard as she worked it slowly over Jenni's leg, trying not to touch skin. She was reminded of a game she used to play with her Dad with a wire and a ring, trying over and over to ease it around the curves without a bell sounding.

Finally the bikini bottoms came clear and Jenni flopped back against the bed.

Kim leaned over her. "Do you want the covers?"

Jenni shook her head. "I'll just lie like this, I think." Her eyes were starting to glaze over. "Those Tylenol are kicking in now. I'm floating."

Kim backed off. "I'll shut the door. I wouldn't want Joe to accidentally get an eyeful."

"Joe can look if he wants," Jenni murmured, but she was starting to drift now.

"I'll come see how you are in a couple of hours."

"You're a sweetheart."

Kim paused at the door, looking back at the unbelievable perfection of Jenni lying across the sheet. The undersides of her heavy breasts were pale, but not as white as her hips where the bikini bottoms had been, and Kim guessed Jenni sometimes went topless. Sighing, she closed the door softly.

Joe was sitting at the kitchen table drinking coffee.

"There's fresh made if you want some."

Kim poured herself a mug and added cream.

"How is she?" Joe asked.

"Okay, I think."

He looked across the table at her. "How about you?"

"I'm fine too, Joe."

She knew Joe was on edge, hyped up by the sudden emergency, but also she imagined because he was turned on. Kim wondered if she should take him to the small second bedroom, but somehow that didn't feel right. The house seemed too confining. She knew Joe needed to let off steam some other way.

"What about you?" Kim asked. "How are you?"

He shook his head. "I don't know. That gave me a hell of a scare."

"She's fine, Joe." Kim reached across for his hand. "Why don't you get out? You said you wanted to hire one of those kayaks. Go do something manly, work it out of your system."

"I don't want to leave you here on your own."

"I won't be on my own. Jenni's upstairs. Besides, I think this has worn me out too. I want to curl up and sleep for an hour. So go, work those gorgeous muscles and come back for dinner."

"Are you sure, babe?"

Kim nodded. "We'll eat around seven. That should give you enough time to work off whatever's ailing you."

Kim knew exactly what was ailing Joe, but she thought it better for that idea to remain unspoken, for the moment.

Chapter 10

Kim jerked awake from a wild dream and looked around, only slowly coming up from the hot place she had been. Her book had fallen closed beside the lounger and her body was vibrating with the sudden jolt of waking.

She sat up and washed her hands across her face, glanced up at the sun. Time to go in anyway.

She picked up her book and discarded t-shirt and walked up on the porch, not bothering to pull her top back on, holding the cotton against her breasts although it was no cover at all. Her breasts were ultra-sensitive again after sleeping, and she wondered idly if it was because the sun had been on them or if there was some other reason. Her nipples had dried up now Ami was asleep. They seemed to respond to her daughter's mere presence. Kim smiled at the thought of Ami and a wash of pure love coursed through her.

In the kitchen she made herself a long drink, made a second and wandered upstairs to the bedroom to see how Jenni was and ask if she needed anything. The bedroom door was not fully closed and Kim pushed it gently, not wanting to disturb the other woman if she was still sleeping.

Jenni lay on top of the bed, sprawling to take up all the room, arms thrown wide, legs splayed, her heavy breasts rising and falling. Kim stood in the doorway, unable to take her eyes off the vision displayed before her. Watching, Kim experienced a throbbing between her legs and lifted a finger to touch her left nipple. She was unbelievably sensitive and gave a quiet gasp as the flesh responded to her touch, stiffening and filling. A bead of milk expressed itself and dampened her fingertip.

Jenni stirred, letting her breath out in a long sigh, twisting one way then the other. She lifted a hand to her face and scratched her cheek. Her eyes opened and stared up at the ceiling before noticing Kim standing in the doorway.

"Oh." Her voice was furred by sleep. "Have you been there long?" She made no move to cover herself, content to display her perfect body to Kim, or unselfconscious enough not to be aware she was displaying.

"Not long." Kim leaned against the edge of the door. "I brought you a drink, or do you want to sleep some more? How's the leg?"

Jenni rubbed her nose and shook her head. "I won't sleep again tonight if I do. The leg's fine now, I think. I really ought to get up." She made no move, instead stretching, arching her back and smiling with pleasure.

Kim straightened and moved into the room. She placed the drinks on the nightstand, turned to the bed, hesitated, sat.

"Are you sure you're okay, Jenni?" She looked into the other woman's eyes, and they both knew the question was not as casual as Kim made it sound.

"I'm good," Jenni said. "How come you and Joe have such a perfect marriage? What's your secret? Tell me, please." Jenni grinned, trying to make a joke of her words.

"We're not so perfect."

"You seem to be from where I am."

Kim pulled a sad face and put her hand on Jenni's right ankle. For a moment Jenni tensed, then relaxed, as though making a conscious decision to let things go where they would.

"I've got a question for you," Kim said.

"Shoot."

"Why is a woman as beautiful as you still hanging around with a loser like your husband?"

Jenni laughed softly, her body stretching once more as though sleep still lingered within her bones and needed to be eased loose. "You overestimate me, Kim. Life's never as easy as it seems. Joe said the same thing to me and I'll give you the same answer I gave him. I'm not beautiful, and I don't have too many options."

Kim shook her head, found her fingers had started to lightly stroke up and down along Jenni's leg, never straying more than six inches from her ankle, but moving in soft trails over the smooth skin. Kim had no idea when she had started to perform the movement, but it felt good to touch the other woman. The tingle came again between her legs. Her eyes dropped from Jenni's face to take in her breasts. Her gaze lingered, openly looking, and as though in response she saw Jenni's nipples fill and lengthen, lifting out from the dark aureole surrounding them. Kim had draped her t-shirt over her shoulder, a token effort to cover herself, but she knew it had settled between them and her breasts were now on display.

"Are you ready to try?" Kim asked. "You can leave him if it's what you want."

"I do want things," Jenni said. "I want kids. Like you. I envy you so much with Ami. She's so gorgeous I want to eat her up."

Kim laughed. "Don't do that. You can have babies with someone else. Maybe it's Mark's fault you can't get pregnant."

"It isn't that simple." Jenni rolled over and lay on her belly, dislodging Kim's hand from her leg.

Kim looked down, studying Jenni's ass, laid her hand back on Jenni's leg, this time higher than before. Kim was nervous, not quite sure what she was really up to, but beginning to form an idea of what she wanted. Butterflies gathered in her stomach. She had never done anything with another woman before. She had played with the idea once or twice, teased Joe a couple of times, the teasing exciting her as well. She knew the scenario aroused Joe, aroused him a lot. She had never touched another woman in the way she wanted to touch Jenni now, but she had never known anyone like Jenni before.

"It can be simple," Kim said. "Leave him, Jen."

"I've got nowhere to go."

"Stay with us."

Jenni gave a bitter laugh. "You don't know Mark. He'd be round here in a second demanding I go back. He's not a nice man, Kim. Not nice at all."

"Joe can take care of us. Besides, I didn't mean here, though you're welcome here too. I meant back home, in New York. Come stay with us in New York."

Jenni rolled on her side to stare at Kim. "You hardly know me." Her breasts swung free as she turned, heavy and curved against the sheets, nipples obscured but the pink circle of her aureole showing.

"Well enough to know how much we like you. Don't underestimate yourself, Jen. Mark's turned you into a mouse, and you're not a mouse." Her hand had reached the back of Jenni's knee, the skin smooth and soft.

"Still." Jenni rested her head on crossed hands. "You don't need me butting in. You're such a tight unit, you and Joe and Ami. You don't need a cuckoo in the nest."

"I'd like it if you came to stay with us," Kim said, and found her voice caught with the emotion coursing through her. "I'd really like it. I know Joe would too."

Kim moved up the bed until she was sitting close to Jenni. The movement caused the t-shirt to fall loose, draping against her thigh before sliding to the floor. Kim moved her hand along the back of Jenni's thigh, slid it high up, not to where she wanted to go, not yet, but closer. Jenni tensed again, as she had when Kim first touched her. Kim waited, and once more Jenni relaxed beneath her fingers. That loosening of the tension excited Kim, made her think the impossible was possible, what she was thinking of might actually happen.

Kim wondered what was going through Jenni's mind. The same thoughts, different thoughts, thoughts of Joe, perhaps? Kim wasn't sure how she felt about that. Not jealous. She imagined the idea of Joe with another woman ought to make her jealous, but something different about Jenni displaced normal emotion.

Jenni sighed, made no reply. Kim didn't know if she had expected one. The butterflies were flapping madly now and she was trying to decide whether to go forward or pull back. How would Jenni react? If Kim moved further, would that be the end of the short friendship that had been developing? Or would she welcome Kim's advances?

Jenni stretched, the movement parting her thighs and Kim smelled the rawness of her, the scent that came with arousal, looked at the perfect skin of her ass, at the tan lines formed by her bikini bottom. She leaned over and kissed Jenni on the side of her hip just where the round curve of her ass formed.

"What are you doing?" Jenni asked, but no shock sounded in her voice, her words soft.

"Kissing your butt." Kim laughed, letting some of her nervous tension loose.

"Why?"

Kim laughed again. "Do you have to ask? You've got maybe the most perfect ass in the world. Why wouldn't I want to kiss it?" Kim leaned down again, kissed once more, further in toward the center, the kiss lasting longer and when she finished she kept her face there, cheek pressed against Jenni's curves.

"Oh... Is that all...?"

"All what?" Kim let her lips tickle Jenni's ass as she spoke.

"As long as that's all you want to do."

"What if I wanted more?" Kim laid her hand high against Jenni's thigh, fingers draping inside her parted legs, almost but not quite touching the bloom of her labia.

"I don't know." Jenni spoke into the sheets. "I've never done anything... you know, with another woman..." She sighed deeply. "You do know I mean, don't you?"

Kim nodded, moved her hand a little. Her finger now pressed lightly against Jenni's pussy. She waited for some indication of resistance, but none came.

"I expect you do this kind of thing a lot, in New York."

Kim laughed, her head shaking gently against Jenni's ass, the globes responding to the movement and Kim took the opportunity to move her hand again so her finger now pressed more firmly. She was sure dampness lay against her finger.

"I've never done anything like this," Kim said, and let another kiss linger on Jenni's ass. She rolled her face sideways, relishing the way Jenni's smooth skin brushed her cheek.

"I don't believe you," Jenni said. "You seem so sure of yourself."

"I'm not sure at all, not about this... only about what I want."

"Oh."

"Do you mind?" Kim asked.

"What, having my ass kissed? And... that other thing you're doing?"

"Yeah, this. Do you mind me doing these things?"

"I don't know."

"You only have to say no, Jen. I won't mind. I'll understand completely. Say no and I'll stop." She pressed her fingers harder against Jenni's slit. The tightness resisted, the fullness of her labia closing her sex to all but a determined finger, and Kim was not yet brave enough to attempt that violation.

"I don't know what to do. I don't know what you want me to say."

"I think you do. You know exactly what you want to do, Jen. You just don't want to say it out loud, but that's okay." She worked her fingers against Jenni's pussy, enjoying the way the curls of pubic hair brushed against the back of her hand. Kim trailed her fingers along the crack of Jenni's ass once more, not pressing too hard where she wanted to.

"It feels odd," Jenni said.

"Good odd or bad odd?" Kim sat up, laid her hand on the soft white skin of Jenni's butt, her fingers curling inside the crack of Jenni's ass. Still no objection came so Kim allowed her hand to drift slowly down between Jenni's thighs again.

"Nn," Jenni said as Kim touched her sex. "Good odd, I guess."

"Yeah?" Kim rubbed her finger along the length of Jenni's slit, definitely slick with juices now. She dropped her other hand to her lap and pressed hard against herself through her bikini bottoms. *These will have to come off*, she thought.

"Mm, yeah," Jenni said.

"You want me to stop?"

Jenni shook her head into the bed.

Kim lay against Jenni and kissed her at the top of her ass, right at the point the deep crack formed from her back. She flicked her tongue out, licked along Jenni's skin, tasting sweat, tasting ocean salt.

"You gotta say it, Jen." Kim allowed her tongue to work down along Jenni's crack. She wasn't sure if she was actually going to perform the act forming in her mind, whether it was too much, whether it would disgust Jenni, but she could always stop or pretend it was a mistake. She put her hands on Jenni's ass cheeks and parted them, exposing the small tight bud nestled there, perfectly pink, perfectly formed. She licked above with her tongue, lightly, once.

"I want you to carry on," Jenni said. "I think I want you to touch me."

"Mm-hm." Kim flicked her tongue again, catching the side of Jenni's asshole and Jenni jerked as though shocked.

"Oh my God!"

"Has anyone ever done this to you before?" Kim flicked her tongue again, letting it linger a moment.

"God no! Has anyone done it to you?"

"Sure," Kim said, voice muffled as she buried herself between Jenni's ass cheeks, her tongue now working against her asshole. "It's good, isn't it?"

"Nn... yeah, I think so. But... it's so dirty."

"No. Your ass is wonderfully clean."

"Doesn't it taste of... you know... of shit?"

Kim laughed softly. "Not at all." She made the tip of her tongue hard and pushed it inside Jenni's asshole.

"Oh my God! Does Joe do this to you?"

"He does."

"Does he like doing it?"

Kim laughed again. "Oh yeah, I do believe he does. *But not as much as I like him doing it to me.* "You're not so innocent, Jen. You've heard about this kind of thing."

"Heard, yeah... I just didn't think – oh Christ!" Jenni yelped as Kim pushed her tongue into her ass and at the same time slid her thumb between her pussy lips and penetrated deep inside.

"You're not allowed to come," Kim said.

Jenni responded as though she had not heard. "Does Joe... does he do anything else to you?"

Kim pecked kisses all over Jenni's ass, tasting the salt of the sea, tasting the essence of the woman. "What kind of things do you mean, Jen?" She re-applied her tongue to Jenni's asshole, pushing slightly, trying to remember how Joe did this to her so she could make it as good.

"Does he only lick you there, or does he... you know, Kim... does he fuck you too?"

"Does Mark fuck you in the ass, Jen?" Kim asked back. She had wetted her finger and pressed it inside Jenni's tight budded asshole. Only as far as the top of her nail yet, but she was beginning to learn exactly why Joe found this such a turn on.

Jenni gasped as Kim's finger probed more deeply, but she also lifted her hips as though wanting more. She shook her head. "Mark hardly fucks me at all. And when he does he's always so angry."

"How can he not want to fuck you? I know Joe'd fuck you all the time if you were his wife."

"Nn," Jenni said as Kim pushed her finger deeper, up to the knuckle now. "Does Joe fuck *you* all the time, Kim?"

Kim turned her hand, the ribbed inner walls of Jenni's ass against her fingertip. "Every day. Sometimes two or three times a day. We love sex, both of us. Love each other."

"You... you're kissing my butt, Kim. You've got your finger..." Jenni stopped, said so softly Kim barely heard, in a small, shy voice, "You've got your finger in my ass. Is that loving Joe?"

"You like?" Kim ignored Jenni's question. "You like my finger in your ass?"

Jenni nodded into the pillows.

"Say it." Kim pressed harder, her finger sliding all the way inside, all the way to the top joint. She could feel the tunnel widening beyond the tight ring of muscle.

"I love it."

"I want Joe to fuck me in the ass." Kim kissed Jenni's cheeks again. She pulled her thighs apart and started to lick along their hollowed inner walls. "But I'm too tight and he's too big."

"You've tried?" Jenni shifted position, making her pussy available when Kim was ready.

"Lots of times. We play with each other. I would love for him to put his cock in my ass, but we can't do it." Kim flicked her tongue across Jenni's slit and felt her jump. "Would you like Joe's cock in your ass, Jen?"

"Ohh... God, Kim, that's so good."

"That wasn't an answer. Tell me, would you like Joe to fuck

you in the ass?"

"I don't know. No. Yes... I don't know."

"Do you want him to try?"

"What are you doing to me," Jenni said, but it was not a protest, more a cry of wonder.

"I want Joe to fuck me in the ass so much, but he can't. He might be able to fuck you while I watch. Would you like that, Jen?"

"Oh God, I'm going to come."

Kim pulled her finger gently from Jenni's ass and sat back. "You're not allowed to come."

"You're kidding me." Jenni moved back against Kim's hand now, all reluctance washed away by lust.

"No. I'm going to work you up and not let you come. I want to see how much you can take."

Jenni rolled over, pulling away from Kim, sliding underneath her and Kim sat up and looked down at the other woman's flushed face. Jenni lifted her legs and lay back with her pussy wantonly exposed, framed by the tuft of dark hair. Jenni slid her hand down and pushed two fingers inside herself.

"No cheating," Kim laughed. She grabbed Jenni's hand and pulled her fingers free. "I'm the only one allowed to touch you there today."

Jenni giggled as they wrestled. Kim played along, enjoying the other woman's body sliding against her own. Their breasts touched and pressed together, and Kim knew she was streaking milk across Jenni's body. Their heads came together, lips close and both slowed, aware that some other boundary was about to be crossed. Jenni stilled and Kim lay against her, their lips almost touching. Jenni's breath was warm and sweet against Kim's face.

Kim angled her head to one side and waited.

Jenni angled her head the other.

Kim lowered her head until her lips brushed against Jenni's, drew back.

She looked into Jenni's dark eyes, saw a glitter deep within. Jenni's hand touched the back of her neck, a soft insistent pressure.

Kim lowered her mouth. Jenni's lips accepted hers, opening, and a tongue explored against her own. Kim parted her lips, allowing the sweet invader to violate her mouth. It had been years since Kim had kissed anyone other than Joe this way. The taste and texture of Jenni's mouth on hers was unbelievable. Fuck, if she had known it was going to feel this good kissing another woman she'd have started a decade sooner.

Jenni's hand slid around, exploring the side of Kim's breast, moved in to find a nipple and Kim jerked at the impossible sensitivity.

She pulled her mouth away and slid down until her lips found Jenni's nipple.

"Kim," Jenni said, wonder in her voice. "I can taste me on your mouth. Oh God... so wicked... Ahh." She gasped as Kim used her teeth lightly on her nipples, stiff and hard now.

Jenni's fingers searched, probing for more and Kim pulled away and slid off the bed.

"Cheating," she said, standing beside the bed, breathing hard. She saw Jenni glance at her chest, looked down at herself, trails of milk streaking the undersides of her small breasts.

"You are so beautiful," Jenni said.

Kim put her fingers in the line of milk and spread it over her breasts. "Sometimes it's a pain in the butt. It's okay out here, but back home I have to put pads on myself."

"It's making me so hot." Jenni rolled over, trying to pull Kim back down.

"No." Kim stepped back. "I told you, I'm only teasing. You're not allowed to touch me."

Jenni's face fell. "Don't you want me to?"

Kim nodded. "So much you wouldn't believe. I'm going to play with you first. Can I play with you, Jen?"

Jenni reached over and caught her fingers in Kim's bikini bottoms. "Take these off first."

Kim laughed and nodded, pulled the slick black material down her legs.

Jenni looked at her exposed mound and said, "You've got a lovely pussy. So delicious shaved like that."

"Thanks. I like yours too."

They both laughed.

"Mine's all hairy," Jenni said.

"That's easy to fix, if you want to."

"No," Jenni shook her head. "How would I explain to Mark?"

"I thought he never fucked you."

"He does, sometimes, but what if he saw I'd shaved myself? How would I explain to him?"

"Would you, if not for that?" Kim asked. Trails of moisture trickled down inside her thighs and it turned her on even more to know that Jenni saw them too.

"I might." Jenni's eyes darted sideways, as if trying to avoid her own wantonness.

"Mm. You've got to promise I can do it for you when you decide to shave your pussy." It was *when* now, not if.

"What are you going to do to me now?" Jenni asked, lying wantonly on the bed.

"Wait there, don't move." Kim went into the hallway, into Ami's room where the infant continued to sleep peacefully. She found what she was looking for. When she returned she had four long strips of silk in her hand.

Jenni's eyes widened. "What are you going to do?"

Kim knelt on the edge of the bed and kissed her again, grasped her left hand and lifted. She wrapped the silk around Jenni's wrist, tying a loose knot, lifted the arm and tied the other end of the silk around the bedpost.

"No," Jenni said, but she offered no resistance when Kim repeated the operation on the other wrist.

Kim turned, straddling Jenni's waist, deliberately exposing her ass and pussy to the other woman. Jenni's lips found her thigh and Kim allowed it for a moment. It was too good to fight. She reached down and tied a strip of silk around one ankle, then the other. She climbed off Jenni and knelt at the foot of the bed, tugged her left leg down and tied it to the bottom bedpost. Jenni offered token resistance, but not enough to prevent her tying the fourth knot.

Kim straightened up and looked down at Jenni spread-eagled on the sheets, her legs parted, her pussy exposed. The flush was pink in her neck and chest and Jenni was breathing hard.

"Now I've got you."

Jenni nodded.

Kim climbed over the end of the bed and crawled up between Jenni's legs. She lowered her head and kissed Jenni on the belly, low down, just above her pubic hair. She wriggled down a little and kissed Jenni directly on her clitoris. She felt Jenni trying to lift her legs and failing, the thin silk drawing tight, stronger than it appeared.

"I've never done this before," Kim said between pecking kisses against Jenni's pussy. "I know what I like, and you're a girl too, so I guess we can work this out."

Jenni pushed up against her mouth and Kim knew the other woman was desperate.

"Jen, how long is it since Mark's made you come?"

"Never."

"You've never come?"

"Not with Mark. I... well, you know what I do."

Kim grinned. "Yeah. I do that too."

"Joe makes you come, doesn't he?"

"Oh yeah," Kim said. She sat back, working Jenni with her fingers, amazed at how slick and oiled her pussy walls were. "That doesn't mean I can't do myself as well. Sometimes it's different, know what I mean? Sometimes we do it in front of each other. He jacks off and watches me doing myself. That's a turn on. I guess you haven't done anything like that either."

"No," Jenni said. "Oh my God... that feels so good."

Kim added a third finger, Jenni tight around them. "I like making myself come for Joe, It's different, wild."

"Ahh." Jenni started a fast tremble and Kim stopped moving her fingers, resting them inside, waiting patiently until the moment passed.

"I think I'm going to use my tongue now," Kim said, sliding down Jenni's flat stomach.

"Uhn," Jenni said.

Forty minutes later Jenni had still not come and Kim knew her own juices were trailing down inside her thighs. She was considering taking pity on Jenni and finishing her off when they both heard the front screen door bang and Joe called out, "I'm home!"

***

Kim rolled from the bed, found her bikini briefs and tugged them on. Her t-shirt was on the floor beside the bed where she had dropped it and she pulled it back over her head.

"What about me?" Jenni hissed.

Kim looked back, grinning. "I'll be back... or maybe I'll send Joe to up untie you."

"What?"

Kim laughed. "Don't worry. How would I explain to him how you got naked and tied up?" She turned away.

"Kim!" Jenni whispered loudly.

Kim stopped.

"Untie me so I can make myself come. I'm so ready if I don't come I think I might go mad."

Kim looked at her, bright eyed and flushed, smiled and went out, closing the door behind her.

She left Jenni on her own for ten minutes. Joe wanted to go through to the bedroom to change, but Kim said Jenni was still asleep and anyway it was his turn to give Ami her bath, and she wanted to change herself before dinner. When she returned to the bedroom Jenni was thrashing on the bed still trying to get loose. Kim stood at the end of the bed and waited for her to stop moving.

"You're in such big trouble," Jenni said, no soft edge to her voice now.

"I don't think so." Kim walked around the bed, grabbed a handful of Jenni's thick hair and kissed her hard. Jenni tried to bite back and Kim pulled away.

"Let me loose," Jenni said. "I need to pee real bad. Would have served you right if I'd peed all over your bed."

"Go ahead, I'd like to watch you."

Jenni looked at Kim like she had lost her mind. "Please."

Kim nodded. "You're not gonna do anything stupid, are you? I was only playing."

"Promise." Jenni sounded subdued, worrying Kim she had gone too far.

She reached to the top of the bed and pulled the knot tying Jenni's left arm. It came loose, the other end of the silk still wrapping her wrist. Jenni reached over and released the other arm herself. Kim went to the foot of the bed and untied her feet. Jenni sat up, rubbing her wrists although they both knew it was only a mock protest, the silk had been tied too loosely to bind.

Jenni rolled off the bed and stood instantly. In one quick move she gripped Kim's arms and pushed her back hard against the wall. Kim gave a small cry, convinced now she *had* gone too far. Jenni used her extra height and strength to pin Kim to the wall and kissed her, Jenni's tongue fighting into her mouth. She dropped to her knees and lifted Kim's leg, buried her face against Kim's pussy. She pulled the bikini bottoms aside and Jenni's tongue entered her and Kim's knees weakened. Jenni rocked back and rose to her full height in front of Kim, stood beautiful and naked, unashamed.

"Two can play games," she said, turning away, then, "Fuck. What am I going to wear?"

Kim recovered her breath and laughed. "Take something of mine from the wardrobe. I don't know what's going to fit you but help yourself. I'm getting changed anyway."

Jenni began flicking through the clothes in the wardrobe, standing naked as Kim stood beside her also deciding what to wear. She had only brought beach clothes, nothing fancy, and finally settled on a loose linen dress that had seen better days. She undressed until she was naked again and then buttoned the dress up the front, leaving three buttons loose at the top, deliberately neglecting any underwear. When she turned to Jenni the other woman was staring at her hungrily.

"What?" Kim asked, blushing.

"You are so sexy," Jenni said, and Kim thought she was going to kiss her again. Instead Jenni turned to the wardrobe and said, "Can I wear this?"

Kim turned to see she was holding up a dark wine-red jersey one piece dress with no buttons or zips but enough stretch to pull over a body. Kim swallowed, imagining how Jenni would look in the dress, fearing Joe was unlikely to glance in her direction all night. She nodded. "Sure."

She sat on the bed and watched Jenni pull the dress over her head and work it down over her naked body. Kim knew the dress was tight on her, on Jenni it was positively obscene. Hardly any curve or dip or crease of her body was not outlined or cupped by the stretched material.

Jenni turned back to the bed and held her arms out. "What do you think?"

Kim gave a nervous laugh. "If Joe doesn't screw you, I think I'm going to have to."

Jenni looked down at herself. "Too much?"

"Of course. But don't change. Let's scare the hell out of him, shall we?"

Jenni looked up and Kim stared into her eyes. This was no longer a game. Kim wasn't sure if the resolution would be reached tonight or not, but soon something was going to break. Jenni would come into the fold of their arms. What happened after that, well, that was for all of them to decide. Kim knew what she wanted, but was afraid if she expressed her thoughts she would scare this vision of loveliness away.

Kim broke the mood, standing and stepping across to hug Jenni.

"You look stunning. Come on, let's go downstairs and pop Joe's eyes out."

Chapter 11

Dinner was a slow, relaxed affair scattered with conversation both light and deep. Joe drove into town to pick up a take-out and they ate Chinese cooked well, opened fortune cookies and laughed over the messages. Jenni pumped Joe to tell her more about his work. She had never met anyone famous, intrigued because Joe did not act as she expected famous people to. He told her just because people recognized your name didn't make you different to anyone else. Except for the money. Jenni could tell from the way he dismissed money he had reached the point where it stopped being important – filthy rich.

Though arousal continued to pulse through her veins, she felt good when the sexual tension in the kitchen drained to a low ebb. Even so she knew she was going to have to stop before getting home to bring herself off. Her pussy tingled from being touched and kissed, and she knew her thighs were damp. Jenni enjoyed the way Joe's eyes ate up her figure in the jersey dress. Her nipples were peaked and showed clearly and she leaned forward so the soft cloth clung against her breasts, dipping into her cleavage, displaying herself for him.

Ami sat in her highchair making sounds and waving her arms, giving an occasional wail when she realized she was missing out on something. Kim lifted her from the chair and laid her to a breast, the cream linen dress perfect for the occasion, requiring only two loosened buttons to expose her nipples to the grasping infant.

Jenni drank more wine than she should, and just after ten Kim said, "You know you don't have to drive, Jen. You can stay here."

The implication of the words sat in the air between all three.

Jenni shook her head. "I have to go. Mark'll be home by midnight. I'll catch hell if I'm not back when he gets there."

There was nothing that needed to be said so they all remained silent, a comfortable silence as though they had known each other many years. Unspoken words filled the room, untaken actions shimmered in the air, each of them hearing the same thing, each aware of the bound emotion running through them.

Ami went to sleep against Kim and Joe pulled her gently away and carried her upstairs to bed.

They moved out to the porch, the night warm and dark, clouds obscuring the stars, light from the porch falling out across the sand. Joe poured brandy into tumblers.

"I can't drink this," Jenni said. "If I get stopped I'll already get a DUI."

"Flash 'em your tits, that'll get you off," Kim said.

"I hardly need to flash anything in this dress." Jenni deliberately pushed her breasts out, knowing the way the cloth caressed them, watching as Joe looked, unable to help himself. She put her quarter full glass on the bleached table and stood. "I'd better go change."

"Take the dress home," Kim said. "Bring it back tomorrow, or keep it if you want."

"Will we see you tomorrow?" Joe asked, trying for a casual tone.

"Maybe. If there's a game on and Mark goes over to his buddies. Let me see."

"You know you're welcome anytime," Kim said.

"I know"

They walked with her across to the pickup and before she opened the door Kim put her arms around Jenni and kissed her on the mouth. When they parted Jenni saw Joe staring, his eyes wide. She put her head on one side. "You want one of those too, Joe?"

Joe glanced at his wife, nodding. "Here comes divorce," he muttered as he slipped his arms around Jenni's waist. He pulled her against him with surprising force, the air escaping Jenni's lungs as much from the animal presence of his body as the embrace. He lowered his mouth to hers and she turned her face up, welcoming him. His tongue sought hers and she parted her lips in willing acceptance. Jenni felt Joe's cock against her belly, a stiff rod straining against his pants, and in the sheer jersey dress Jenni felt almost naked against him. The kiss finally broke and she knew her nipples had grown rigid; they tingled and pulsed, but not as much as her pussy.

With a sigh she climbed into the cab and started the engine. Jenni threw a single wave through the window as she drove up the sandy track toward the spine of the island and town. Once over the ridge she pulled onto grass at the side of the road. Her body flamed, desperate for relief, and she tugged the hem of the dress upward, gathering it around her waist. The smell of her aching pussy filled the cab of the pickup and she knew she didn't need to worry about being disturbed because this was going to take no time at all.

For a few seconds she hesitated, her hand trembling over her stomach, stretching the moment until she could wait no longer. She lowered her fingers to her pussy. God, she was so wet, she could not remember when she had ever been this way before. Her fingertip pressed against her clitoris, erect and proud of its hood, dipped lower and she lifted her right leg over the gearshift and plunged her fingers inside herself with a muffled cry. She tugged at the dress again, above her breasts now, the whole thing wrapped beneath her arms, cool air an electric charge against her body.

"Yes," she grunted, eyes closed, imagining Joe leaning over her. She arched upward; her body curved tight and instantly began to shake. She had never come so fast before, but she had never been aroused for so long without relief. She cried out again, opening her eyes, afraid someone might hear, knowing her cry had been too loud but the night was dark, the sea grass hissing softly all around. Jenni jerked again, trying to push her hand all the way inside her pussy, managing four fingers, almost her whole fist, wanting to curl around the quivering ache inside and hold onto it forever.

Five full minutes passed before she recovered enough to tug the dress back down and drive on.

By the time Mark came home, well after midnight, Jenni had showered and changed into her nightdress. She lay in bed reading. The book the other one of Joe's and she felt a moment's anxiety Mark might see the cover and she closed it and put it in the drawer of her nightstand.

"Did you have a good time?" she asked Mark as he stumbled in. He'd obviously not worried as much as her about driving with too much beer in him.

"Lost to fuckin' Tony again. Don't know how he does it every fuckin' time."

Because he doesn't get wasted, Jenni thought, but said, "Never mind, Mark. You'll get him next time."

Mark dropped his pants and stepped out of them and Jenni saw his cock tenting his shorts. Not much, but then he didn't have much to tent them with. Unlike Joe. For a moment she had a vivid image of Joe standing in the bedroom instead of Mark, and knew if that was the case she would not feel the same disgust she now did.

Mark had never believed much in foreplay. He might have read about it once in Penthouse, but in the same detached, uninterested way he read about places in Europe. Those places existed, but they weren't America so had nothing to do with him.

Jenni let him roll on top of her as he released his cock. His leg parted hers and he fumbled for her entrance. If only he kissed me during sex, Jenni thought, staring past his shoulder at the ceiling, or touched me anywhere at all, touched my breasts, touched my shoulder or neck. Mark entered her quickly, Jenni's earlier arousal still evident in the slickness of her opening. Thankfully Mark was too drunk to notice or wonder why she was so wet; or maybe he believed she really wanted him.

Mark started grunting almost at once, Jenni hoping this would be mercifully short. But she discovered tonight was one of those other nights that were becoming increasingly common; Mark was humiliated after losing his game, Jenni a handy punch bag, and so when his fist landed she rolled her head to one side and pressed her eyes tight shut. Be quick, she prayed. Fuck me and finish quickly.

This time Mark's anger was worse than she had ever known it, a merciless escalation taking place, perhaps still banked up after finding Joe's signature in the book. Gasping, he closed his fingers around her neck and squeezed. Jenny tried to push him away but he released one hand to punch her in the side hard enough to leave a bruise in the morning. His hand came back and he bit her shoulder, drawing blood. His fingers tightened, and when Jenni tried to pull air into her lungs nothing came. The room began to gray out and she heard Mark's grunting fade, as if she was being drawn from him, drifting away... drifting...

Fuck! The thought seared through her brain. I finally find people who really like me and I'm going to be killed in my bed. Fuck, fuck, fuck!

Finish, she cried in her head. Finish and let me live.

Through the dimness she heard a final loud grunt and Mark jerked against her. Done. He rolled away and Jenni finally drew in a gasp of air, her throat sore, her lungs aching. She pulled her nightdress down but didn't dare go clean up yet. She lay listening to Mark's breathing slow. Almost immediately he began to snore, lying on his back with his mouth open.

Jenni slipped from the bed and went through to the small bathroom, wiped herself clean with a damp washcloth and splashed water on her face. Twice in one week, she thought, trying to remember the last time Mark had instigated sex twice in a month, let alone a week. Why now? She shook her head, knowing why. Because he no longer cared what he did to her. Because his business was going down the pan and he didn't know how to stop it. Because anger, not Jenni, offered him comfort.

She turned on the light above the mirror and checked herself over. Finger marks showed red on her neck, but she didn't think they were going to bruise. Which was more than she could say for her ribs. Already a shadow had formed and by morning would be a deep blue. She would have to miss swimming tomorrow, or at least skip swimming with Joe. No way was she going to let them see what Mark had done to her.

Jenni sank to her knees, resting her head against the cold sink and drew air deep into her lungs, grateful she was able to still do so. She thought she might throw up. She tried to recall what she had ever seen in Mark, if she had *ever* seen anything in him. How in hell had she married the man? She had been offered alternatives, other men, although sometimes it was hard remembering their faces and names, as though everything had happened to someone else. She had even enjoyed the sex with some of them.

She put the lid down on the toilet and sat, leaning forward, arms resting on her knees. She closed her eyes and remembered the first time she had sucked a cock. Greg Bingham, a football player. His cock had been thick but not very long and she managed to take it to the root, take it easily even though the tip bumped up against the top of her throat. She had only meant to suck him a little then finish him off with her hand, but he had gripped her hair, holding her head down on his cock and she could not break free; not sure she wanted to break free, because Greg's arousal had aroused her too. She had pushed her fingers inside her panties and rammed them inside herself as Greg pumped into her mouth. He grunted and Jenni got ready but it was a false alarm. She pushed her fingers deeper inside herself and knew she was going to come as well. Greg shuddered and suddenly her mouth filled with his cum, hot and slippery with a metallic salty tang and she still didn't move, swallowing as he ejaculated and then as he filled her mouth a second time she swallowed that too, her heart beating hard at the idea of what she was doing, excited by the power she possessed over him, knowing she wanted to do this again soon. As Greg released his grip on her hair and slumped back Jenni's own climax ripped through her. It wasn't her first, but it was the best so far.

Jenni sighed and shook her head. Greg had gotten what he wanted. He never asked her out again, but he did put word around. Jenni Clarke gave great head. She had been Clarke back then, somehow the remembrance of her maiden name almost bringing tears to her eyes. One blow job and she'd managed to get a reputation. She hated the reputation, but hated herself more. She guessed that was why, when Mark picked her and didn't want to stick his cock down her throat – not that he was big enough to do that – she had settled for him. Yes, she thought, settled was the right word. She had been seeking a haven from her reputation, a reputation she didn't deserve. Or maybe she did. Jenni knew her sex drive was something almost to be feared. She feared it now. She wanted Joe, and she wanted Kim. She wanted to writhe in sweaty abandon between the two of them. Her mind spiraled down among images of cunt and cock and ass and despite the ache in her side and the pain in her heart her body responded. She was lost, completely lost, and she started to cry because she didn't know what to do.

Chapter 12

Jenni didn't come around Saturday, the day after their dinner, the day after Kim had tied her up, and sometime during the day Joe looked at Kim without saying anything. Kim looked away wondering if what she had done had scared her off. Ami offered rescue by demanding attention.

In the afternoon Joe swam alone, Kim telling him to look out for jellyfish. He was gone a long time and after Ami went to sleep Kim dozed on the sun lounger, waking to see him walking up the beach, the languor in his body showing how hard he had swum. Joe stripped his trunks off on the porch and toweled dry. The beach was quiet, no one in sight, and Kim rolled her head and studied him, his cock hanging long between his legs, his balls round and full. For some perverse reason she had not let him fuck her since Jenni left even though she wanted him. Now, seeing him half erect she wanted him with a sudden rage. She rolled off the lounger and without a word took his hand and led him inside and upstairs. She tugged her bikini top up and left it loose above her breasts, knelt on the bed, presenting herself to him. Joe pulled her bikini briefs to one side, her pussy instantly soaking his cock as he thrust into her, one long movement that placed the head of his long cock right up against her cervix. Joe closed his hands around her waist, thumbs touching along her spine, fingertips almost touching over her navel.

Kim trembled, about to come almost instantly, put her head down as Joe filled her, a delicious ache pinpointing inside and blooming outward. She yelled into the pillow, arching back against him, letting him knead her breasts as milk spurted against his hands.

When she stopped shaking she pulled away and turned, taking him in her mouth, taking half his length, as much as she could manage. She pushed the tip of her tongue down inside his central slit, pushed him on his back and jerked his thighs apart.

She sat on her heels and lifted her hand to her mouth. Joe lay on his back, knees apart, watching her. His cock bounced with each heartbeat, bouncing fast, thick and meaty and long, dark threaded veins showing, the head bulbous and smooth. Pre-cum oozed from the central slit, gathered and coated him.

Kim pushed her index finger into her mouth, licking it, soaking it with saliva, enjoying Joe watching her, enjoying him knowing what she was about to do. She withdrew her finger and held it over Joe's cock. A trail of spit dripped on his cock and she saw him jerk as it touched him. She pushed his legs wider with her knees and inserted her finger back into her mouth. She dipped down and licked his smooth round balls. He had started shaving his balls for her years ago, resisting the rest but happy to leave them smooth and stippled. She sucked on them, her finger still in her mouth, the movement awkward but exciting. When she drew it out she pushed hard beneath him. Joe, aware of what she wanted, lifted himself and she rolled him on his side. She gripped his cock in one hand, rolled over him and put her wet finger on the dimple of his ass and pressed. Joe's asshole opened and she pushed harder, pushed until her finger was embedded to the top joint.

"You like this, don't you, Joe?" She whispered into his ear, her other hand stroking his cock.

Joe nodded.

"Tell me," she said, biting his ear. She rubbed his cock faster, pushed her finger in and out of his ass.

"I like it," he said.

"What do you like, Joe?" She bit his neck, trembling hard, turning herself on too and she wondered if she would come just doing this; she believed she might.

"I like when you put your finger in my ass," Joe said.

She kissed his shoulder. "You know what I'm going to do when we get back to New York?"

"What are you going to do, Kim?"

She had played with the idea for a while now, something wicked and wild. "I'm going to find a sex shop. Not some sleazy one, but a nice place. I'm going to buy one of those strap on cocks. Why am I going to do that, Joe?"

He was breathing harder now. "Why?"

Kim pushed Joe's leg up with hers, sat herself on his thigh so her bare pussy pressed against her hand, the hand which had a finger in Joe's ass.

"I'm going to get one so I can fuck you in the ass, Joe." She pulled her finger out, pressed her pussy against his ass. Pressing hard, flattening her pussy lips against him, Joe's wrinkled asshole pressed back against her clit and she started to hump him. "Like this, but harder. I'm going to fuck your ass so good you'll never want anything else."

"Yes," Joe gasped.

"Yes what?"

"Yes, I want you to fuck my ass."

Kim humped against him, another climax gathering inside. She rubbed Joe's cock, leaning over so she could watch when he came. She loved to watch him come, loved the thick jets of semen shooting from his cock. She loved everything about this man, every tiny little part of him. She pumped harder, wishing she was fucking him now, wishing she had a cock she could thrust into his pretty little ass.

"Fuck me," Joe grunted.

"Yes, I'll fuck you."

"Fuck me now," Joe cried and Kim leaned over as he ejaculated, splashing over the sheets and she laughed as her own pleasure peaked.

"Fuck you," she whispered, pumping, jerking and trembling. "Fuck you... fuck you..."

She collapsed on top of him, her hand slippery, the sheets once more soiled. She lay scissored against Joe, her pussy pressed against his balls, their legs tangled and greedy. She wanted more than was possible, somehow always wanting more.

Without moving she said, "I want to ask you something, Joe."

He lifted his head and looked down at her. "That sounds serious."

She laughed softly. "Maybe."

Joe waited, said, "What?"

"What would you think if I said I wanted to fuck a

woman?"

Joe went quiet, lying still beside her and she could almost hear the whirr of his thoughts.

"I know we've joked about this," Joe said.

"Have we? Did you think I was joking?"

"You weren't?"

"Maybe," Kim said. "Or maybe I've never found the right woman before."

"You're talking about Jenni, aren't you?"

Kim nodded, realized he would not see her face and said, "Yes, Jenni. How would you feel if I told you I wanted to fuck Jenni?"

Joe was quiet a long time, and when he spoke he said, "Just you and Jenni?"

Kim laughed and sat up, sitting across his hips. "You got such a dirty mind. No wonder I love you so much."

"No idea what you mean." Joe trying for innocence and failing.

Kim leaned over and kissed him, lifted his hands to her tender breasts. "I almost fucked Jenni the other day when you were out." She watched his face for a reaction, but his cock, not his face, gave her an answer, stiffening against her thigh, sliding, still slippery, to lodge against her hip.

Kim leaned down again and whispered, "I tied her to this bed and played with her, Joe. I kissed her, like I kiss you. I kissed her tits and put my finger in her ass and I licked her pussy. I wouldn't let her come and she was begging me to. She wanted me to fuck her." Kim put her head next to Joe's ear and whispered, "Like she wants you to fuck her. She wants us both to fuck her. Do you want to fuck her, Joe?"

He nodded. "I want to fuck her, Kim."

She sat back and looked at him, played with his cock, enjoying its slick hardness. She reached across him, Joe kissing her nipples as she stretched. A bottle of baby oil sat on the nightstand and Kim retrieved it, flicked the cap up and dripped oil onto Joe's cock, spread it over his length, dripped more on until he was slippery and slick. She wriggled so he found her pussy and then settled on him, their bodies still awkward but better for that, more fun when it wasn't so easy.

"I like her a lot," Kim said.

"So do I."

"No, you don't understand. I *really* like her. I asked if she wanted to come live with us."

"You what? Christ, Kim, what were you thinking of?"

She realized she had gone too far... until she saw his eyes. She grinned. "You want that too, don't you?"

"Oh fuck, Kim. We can't do that to her. She's not a toy we can play with, she's a grown woman with her own life and needs."

"I know." She moved against him, aroused by the way he filled her, by the way his oiled cock moved easily inside her pussy, aroused by his arousal. "I don't mean I want to do anything like that, don't want to make her do anything she doesn't want. She's so strong; you can see the strength in her. She doesn't belong here. I want her to live with us. Not like some extra part, not like some plaything, but to be with us, fully with us."

"God Kim, you can't suggest that and expect an answer. I need to think about something as big as that." Joe groaned, a flush spreading over his chest and neck. He was pumping hard against her, lifting her from the bed on each stroke and she loved the way she was nothing to him, his strength overpowering her weight as though she were made of feathers.

"I want you to know that what you feel is okay with me, Joe. I want you to have her too. I want you to do this to her. I want you to do everything to her... and I think she wants that too. Oh fuck, Joe, like that, do me like that babe!"

He gripped her waist again, pulling and lifting, thrusting half sideways into her as she straddled him. Kim tipped over, felt the wave crest and burst inside her belly and she shook and flopped at the same time, draping herself over Joe, pulling his cock free of her pussy so it slapped against her ass and she grinned and pressed down, his cock meeting the resistance of her ass and she lifted off then pressed harder, grabbing his cock and forcing herself down against him. She grabbed the oil and reached around, twisting and squeezing hard. Clear oil spat from the bottle and she felt it splash across her ass, felt it pool between her cheeks.

"What are you doing?" Joe's voice was hoarse.

"What do you think? Try, Joe, try for me babe."

Kim pressed her slippery ass down against his cock, pain flooding sharply through her, but it was good too and Joe stared wide eyed as she forced her weight down hard, driving him inside. For the first time her ass opened to his cock and Joe slipped inside her sweet pink anus. The pain was sharp and sweet but she was coming again, the pain and the sensation of being filled cancelling each other out, leaving joy he was finally doing this thing she had wanted for so long.

"Oh babe," Joe groaned.

"Do it," Kim hissed, sweat breaking across her face. "Fuck me, Joe." She pressed down again and more of his cock split her apart.

"Ahh!" Joe cried out as he spasmed inside her, the pain and the wonder making her head spin, but he was shooting inside her ass. She had wanted this for so long, but God it hurt, she couldn't stand the pain long but she wanted it too much, wanted Joe to spill inside her ass and she pressed down so he could penetrate her further, spilling inside her again, his semen lubricating her passage and making progress easier, but still it hurt so much. Kim was trembling with the pain, but Joe finished ejaculating and started to soften. The pain eased, faded, still a shard of glass splitting her in two but now she was full, fulfilled. Trying to keep him inside she leaned over and kissed him, licked the sweat from his cheek.

"What the fuck was that!" Joe moaned.

"What I've always wanted, my love." His cock slipping from her now, even that withdrawal burning and Kim pushed him free and slumped back holding her stomach.

"I didn't think we could do that," Joe said, breathing hard.

"Nothing's impossible if you want it enough."

"I hurt you, babe."

She nodded. "I wanted you more than the hurt, Joe. Much, much more."

"Oh my God."

Kim nodded. "I don't think we'll be able to try again for a while." She giggled.

"Emergency room?" Joe asked, concerned now.

"Not quite. Close, but not quite."

"I'm sorry," he said, rolling over as he cradled her in his arms.

Kim shook her head. "I wanted that, Joe, you know I did. It wasn't about you. I've always wanted that and I needed it now, more than the pain." She kissed him on his eyelids, his forehead, the tip of his nose, his lips. "I love you, Joe."

"I love you too, Kim."

"You better had after what we just did," she said, and slapped him on the chest.

Chapter 13

Jenni didn't come around the following day either, and Kim began to worry she had scared her off, the passion too strong from her, or maybe too strong in Jenni. Tuesday morning they went to the small super-mart in town, and when Kim and Joe turned into the middle aisle they almost ran straight into Jenni. Ami, happily sitting in the baby seat of their trolley recognized Jenni and gave a little squeal, her pudgy arms waving to be picked up.

"Jenni," Kim said, reaching for the taller woman's hand, stopping as Jenni gave a tiny shake of her head and her eyes flashed an unmistakable warning.

Joe nodded at her and went to push the trolley past.

"Who's this?" A man's voice, gruff but not deep enough to carry much menace, the voice of someone who smokes and drinks too much.

"This is Joe and Kim Fransiscus," Jenni said, turning to the man, her shoulders stiff. "I told you about them, Mark. They're staying in the Bradley place on the beach."

"The writer," Mark said. His eyes were unwelcoming and even at eleven in the morning Joe smelled whiskey on his breath.

Jenni flinched as her husband turned to her and Joe's muscles tensed, ready to defend her.

"We need to get on," Mark said, not looking at Joe.

Jenni glanced at them and offered a lift of her shoulders. "I'll see you around. Come on Mark, we need steak."

"Too right." He glared at Joe but it was a fake look and carried no menace. Joe was surprised at the man, having built him into some giant hate figure in his mind. Mark was whip thin with dark, lank hair already starting to recede. He wore stained overalls and had not shaved for a couple of days. He was not tall or strong or mean only sad and weedy. How in hell, Joe wondered, had someone as wonderful as Jenni ended up with this man?

They moved on and, after checking over her shoulder to make sure they had gone, Kim whispered, "So that's the dreadful Mark?"

"Looks like," Joe said.

"What the hell?" Kim said.

Joe looked at her. "I was thinking exactly the same thing myself."

Ami gave a grunt and tried to climb out of the baby seat toward a display of bright cereal. Joe looked down at her and plopped her back into the seat. "You think she's ready for solids yet?"

"She better not be," Kim said. Feeding Ami was one of her secret pleasures, Joe knew.

"You can still feed her, babe, but I think she might be ready for something more substantial."

Kim gave him a stern look. "You think these aren't substantial enough, Joe?" She crossed her arms under her breasts and lifted them. As usual, she was leaking through her t-shirt but didn't seem to care if anyone saw.

Joe laughed, turned serious as they walked on. "I didn't like him."

"Surprise, surprise," Kim said, her voice low so as not to carry beyond the aisle. "You've only been aching to fuck his wife all week. Did you expect to like him?"

"Yeah, well." Joe flushed. "Even so, I still don't like him. He doesn't appreciate what he's got."

"I know she's beautiful, inside and out, and I love her as much as you, Joe, but we'll be going home in a few weeks. What did you think was going to happen, did you really think we were going to ask her to come home with us?" Even though Kim had expressed exactly that same thought, now it seemed as though she was backing away from the idea.

Joe studied the cartons of milk, making a show of deciding which one they should buy.

Kim stopped and put her hands on her narrow hips. "You did, didn't you."

He glanced at her. "Did what, babe?"

Kim stared at him. "You want to ask her to come back with us, don't you?"

"Of course not. Besides, it was you put the idea in my head."

Kim continued to stare at him, her head to one side. Ami leaned forward and tugged at a bag of nappies, trying to lift them into her lap, totally absorbed in the task.

"You really do want to," Kim said.

Joe turned away, went in search of coffee. Kim left Ami in the trolley and followed.

"For fuck's sake, Joe, I appreciate her as much as you do, but what the hell are you thinking?"

He sighed and stopped pretending he was trying to decide between Columbian or Java ground. "It was only an idea, Kim. *Your* idea," he stressed.

She stared at him, said, "I wasn't serious, Joe. You do realize that, don't you? I wanted your cock in my ass and I was out of control. Wow. She's bowled you over, hasn't she?"

Joe shook his head.

"Should I be worried?" Kim asked, her voice taking on a steely edge.

"Of course not," Joe said. "You're the only one I love, babe."

Kim stared hard at him. "Jesus. I need to think about this. It was a joke, Joe. Something to turn you on. Turn us both on."

She turned away and went to the trolley, took the pack of razor blades from Ami who had pulled them from the Aladdin's cave of goodies in the trolley. She pushed the trolley past Joe, staring hard at him as she went and after she passed Joe turned and followed, his head down. He tried hard to think what to say, because Kim was right. When she had raised the idea, joke or not, though he hadn't thought she was joking when she said it, the idea had burned into his brain. He had been thinking ever since about what life could be like, what it would mean if Jenni came back with them to New York. He might pretend to himself they were helping her find work, helping her find an apartment, but in his heart Joe knew he wanted her with *them*.

He wanted the three of them to live together, a unit, a triad of love and lust. He didn't want to lose Kim, but he didn't want to give up Jenni either. He knew the decision was not his to make, not Kim's, although he was convinced she wanted Jenni as much as he did. Kim would accept Jenni because he had seen the way she acted with her, as enamored by her as he was himself. It would be up to Jenni. Was she able to push past the sense of guilt and worthlessness her husband had instilled in her and make the break? He wanted to think she was capable of making the decision, but he didn't know, not for sure.

He followed behind Kim, watching her shoulders tense and a thought crystallized in his mind. Kim was pissed because he had caught her out. She wanted Jenni with them as well. Her apparent touchiness was a front to mask her true feelings. Joe knew Kim too well for her to hide something this huge from him, and as he pushed the trolley and Ami smiled up at him he grinned back and gave her a big wink.

***

Friday night Joe lay naked in bed watching Kim undress and said, "I don't know if I should ask this or not, but why are we not having sex anymore?"

Kim stopped with her panties off one leg but still on the other. She looked at Joe. "I want to wait."

"What if I don't?"

"It'll be worth it." Kim dropped her panties and crossed to the bed in all her glorious nakedness. Joe got hard just looking, harder because he had not come since Sunday. Kim had to be feeling the same because if anything she wanted sex even more often than he did.

Automatically Joe lifted his arm and Kim snuggled underneath, her hot body pressing against him causing his cock to fill even more. His erection was obvious, tenting the thin sheet.

"I'm not being cruel, babe. You know what we're waiting for, don't you?"

"Jenni," Joe said. They had talked about her all week, Kim's reluctance in the super-mart completely gone.

Kim nodded against Joe and laid her hand on his chest, her fingertips idly playing with the sparse hairs growing along the center.

"Do you think she's going to come back?"

"I don't know," Kim said. "I really don't know."

"How long are we going to wait before you let me fuck you?"

Kim laughed against him. "Sunday, Joe. If Jenni doesn't come round tomorrow you can fuck me Sunday. You can even try my ass again if you want, it's stopped hurting now."

Joe kissed her brow. "I'm not gonna hurt you that way again."

She kissed him back and wriggled, her body softening as it relaxed. "I wish I wasn't so tight. I really want you to fuck my ass, Joe. Maybe now we know we *can* do it we can try again, keep trying till we get it right."

"I'm not sure, babe. I don't mind if we don't."

"I know you don't mind, but I do. The idea of you fucking my ass turns me on so much. Turned me on, when we did, even if it did hurt like hell. I'll never forget that, Joe, even if it's our only time ever."

"There's plenty else we can do." Joe had loved the act as well, the thing they had both wanted for so long and had begun to believe was not possible. When Kim had opened to him, even if for a moment, he had been unbelievably turned on. No wonder he'd come so fast.

"We won't wait till Sunday," Kim said. "If she doesn't come round tomorrow you can come all over me." Kim grinned, thinking about how much she would enjoy that as well. She pulled loose from his arm and rolled away. Joe followed, hugging her close, his body sensitive to every minute touch of her skin.

"We're kind of assuming Jenni's going to want this too, aren't we?"

"She wants it," Kim said. "She wants it as much as we do."

"So we're okay on this now? No jealousy?"

"Not from me," Kim said. "How about you?"

"Me? Why would I be jealous? I'd be getting every man's

fantasy."

"Suppose I discovered I liked women more than men? How would you feel?"

Joe was silent for a while. Finally he said, "Is that likely?"

"I don't suppose," Kim said. "But you do have to admit she is one hot package."

"Mm."

"It's your turn tonight, isn't it?" Kim asked.

Joe nodded against her shoulder. "Afraid so."

"Good. The bottle's in the fridge. Ten seconds in the microwave and test it first."

"I know."

"Just in case."

"I know." Joe kissed her shoulder, hoping his boner would go down before Ami woke him at three for a feed. She always slept well, but three was her regular ungodly hour to drag her parents from sleep; that deep, dark sleep of the small hours.

Chapter 14

Jenni drove down to the back of the Harper place, pulling in at her usual spot. Her breath came too fast, her entire body vibrating. When she lifted her hands from the wheel they shook. Not only nerves, though that was a large part; it was more than nerves, more than a single emotion running through her veins. In fact, nerves were at the bottom of the pile. At the top, sitting raw, red and rampant sat her lust.

Jenni closed her eyes, listening to the inner voice for a moment. Yes, it spoke loudly. She arched her back and pushed against the vinyl seat. She had gone deliberately through her wardrobe that morning, and although a casual glance would not reveal it she had chosen both items she wore as carefully as if going to a prom. One ragged tank top and one pair of even older cut-off denims. The denims she hadn't taken out in almost ten years. They were faded almost white, a tear in the back showing a crescent of bare ass. She wore nothing beneath, nor beneath the top which was also faded pale. She was surprised they fitted; barely fitted. Both bordered on too small, exactly the effect she wanted. As she pressed down against the seat the thick seam on the denims pushed against her pussy and she almost purred with the wave of pleasure it sent coursing out from her loins. Thank God the material was heavy enough to mask her arousal; anything finer would already be giving away her secret with a large damp stain. Her nipples stiffened against the thin cotton and Jenni knew they were obvious to anyone who looked. She was hoping someone was going to look.

After Mark left for work and she had cleared the breakfast plates she showered in their tiny bathroom. Afterward, taking one of Mark's disposable razors and sitting on the edge of the bath, she had carefully trimmed the hair from around her labia. She had drawn the blade higher, shaving away the edges of her pubic hair, each stroke edging closer to removing everything until she had to stop herself, not yet ready for the complete package like Kim, but even the little she removed had almost caused her to come. It was not merely the sensation of the sharp blade running over her pussy lips or the touch of her fingers as she massaged the shaving foam in, but the idea, the taboo nature, to her, of what she was doing. The shakes had started before she finished, almost preventing her completing the task her hand was trembling so much. She had rinsed herself with the shower head, biting down on her lip as water pulsed against her pussy and she forced herself to turn the spray off. She had wanted to come so much she had almost given in. She had to wait. Kim and Joe would make her come. She wanted that completely, wanted that more than anything.

Letting her breath out all at once Jenni opened the squealing pickup door and walked barefoot around the house. It was late September with not a single change over today so Jenni was early. Kim and Joe were the only people still in residence in the dozen large beach houses spread along this piece of shoreline. The air was cooler as the heat of summer leaked away, but the sea would still be warm if they ever got as far as swimming today. Jenni carried a small plastic bag containing her mismatched bikini and the beautiful jersey dress Kim had loaned her. Jenni had tried to make herself wait, not wanting them to sense her desperation but by eleven she had cleaned the kitchen three times and gone back into the bathroom twice with the intention of removing the rest of her bush and had decided she had to get out, go down to the beach house and whatever fate awaited her there.

Jenni had forced herself to stay away all week, hoping Mark's anger and suspicion might fade, wondering if her own infatuation was shallow enough to be dismissed. Almost wishing the feelings raging inside would leave and she could return to her life – lousy as it was. She had waited for the fresh bruises to fade, waited for sanity to reassert itself, but although the dark shadows left her skin the lust remained and eventually she knew she had to return to this house on the beach, return to the couple she wanted, the couple she needed, whatever the outcome was going to be.

The seam along the crotch of her jeans rubbed against clean pussy lips with every step she took and Jenni allowed her awareness to focus there at last. God, she hoped she hadn't misread their intentions. She mentally shook herself. No, of course she hadn't. How would they react to her slutty appearance, she wondered? Even after the words both had spoken to her, after the things Kim had done to her, Jenni lacked faith in her looks and her body, failed to see what was glaringly obvious to everyone other than Mark.

***

Joe sat on the porch bouncing Ami on his lap. His daughter was unsettled today, a new tooth popping through, her gum sore. They had rubbed Dr Shepherds on her gum which had helped a little, but she was still out of sorts. She had woken Joe at two that morning and again at five and he was woozy from lack of sleep.

Ami stopped making the little moaning noise she had been practicing for the last hour and when Joe glanced up to discover what had distracted her he saw Jenni walking across the gap between the houses. His breath stopped, guilt surging through him as he grew instantly hard, the response feeling wrong with his daughter standing on his legs but it was nothing he could stop, a pure reaction. Jenni looked unbelievable. She waved and Joe balanced Ami and lifted one hand and waved back, gripped Ami's wrist and waved her hand as well. Jenni stopped below the porch, grinning. She stuck her hands in the back pockets of the cut-off jeans, a move designed to push her hips forward and breasts out. How in hell she managed to get her hands in the pockets Joe didn't know, because if they were any tighter she'd be wearing them inside her skin. The legs had been cut roughly as though with a knife, strands of denim hanging down against her thighs. The waistband scooped low, displaying a stretch of tanned skin between the bottom of her tank top and the start of the copper buttons running down the front of the shorts. The denim tugged tightly between Jenni's legs, outlining the full lips of her pussy. The thin tank top failed enchantingly to hide the peaks of her nipples and it was more than obvious she wore no bra beneath. One strap was torn half through, drifting down off her shoulder.

"Ah!" Ami cried, holding her arms out and the look on Jenni's beautiful face changed, the heat of lust fading to be replaced by joy and she reached up over the porch rail as Joe handed Ami over. Legs bicycled and Ami grabbed Jenni's hair, pulling hard enough to hurt but Jenni only hugged her against her shoulder and kissed her head.

"We've missed you this week," Joe said. "Has everything been okay?"

Jenni nodded. "Mark's been a bit wired. He kept asking about you after we met in the super-mart."

"What did you tell him?"

"The truth," Jenni said, staring into his eyes.

"The truth?"

"Sure. You're renting the beach house. I see you around. That's the truth, isn't it?"

"Ah," Joe said. "*That* truth."

"Yeah, that one"

"How long can you stay?" Joe gazed back at her, wondering if the hunger showed in his eyes as it showed in Jenni's.

"Same as last week. Mark'll be bowling so I can stay for dinner. If I'm invited that is." Jenni's cheeks flushed and for a moment she appeared embarrassed at her assumption.

"Of course you're invited."

"Don't you need to ask Kim?" Jenni came up on the porch and sat in one of the bleached wooden chairs across from Joe. Kim wriggled against her front and put a pudgy hand directly against her breast. It was all just something to play with as far as she was concerned.

"We talked," Joe said. "Stay as long as you like. Whenever you like." He watched as Ami grabbed the neck of Jenni's tank top and tugged downward, revealing the soft upper swell of her breasts, the deep valley of her cleavage. He let his eyes drift openly over her body, down to her thighs. She had lifted one leg over the arm of the chair as though wanting to display herself to him, and the movement stretched the denim so tight he glimpsed the outer edges of her labia peeking out. He stared, a jolt of arousal rushing through him as he saw she was completely free of hair. He wondered if it was uncomfortable; the jeans way too small, way too tight to be anything other than uncomfortable. Not that he was complaining.

***

Jenni and Joe started as the screen door slammed. Kim caught the look on Joe's face as he stared at Jenni and smiled. Jenni's neck and chest was flushed pink and she went back to playing with Ami to cover her obvious arousal.

"What's wrong with her today? She's not herself." Kim heard Jenni cough in an attempt to clear the lust from her voice.

"She's teething." Kim sat next to Joe and brushed her hand against his arm. She wore bikini pants and the blue cover-up but no bikini top, and as the wind caught and lifted the feather-light material her breasts appeared uncloaked, then re-covered but still visible.

"Poor little thing." Jenni hugged Ami to her.

Kim laughed. "You wouldn't say that if you had those tooth stumps gnawing at your tits. God, she's going to need feeding again soon."

"I'll give her a bottle," Joe said. "You don't need to be a martyr."

Kim smiled gratefully. "I think I might just let you."

"Can I?" Jenni asked, shyly. "I'd like to feed her."

"Sure," Kim said. "Are you and Joe going swimming? Did you bring your stuff?"

"Of course." Jenni leaned forward, her breasts dipping inside the tank top. She pushed a plastic shopping sac across the table. "I brought your dress back too. I washed it."

"You didn't need to." Kim opened the top of the bag and looked inside. The jersey dress lay inside neatly folded, the smell of the same conditioner Jenni used on their sheets escaping. "I want you to keep it."

"I can't do that. It's expensive."

"I want you to keep it," Kim said. "It looks a whole lot better on you than it does me."

"I doubt that," Jenni said, but she flushed again, bit the

corner of her lip. "I'd like to see it on you, Kim." Her eyes came up, brazen now.

Kim laughed. "Maybe we'll have a fashion show later on. Me and you, we can drive Joe wild."

"I like the sound of that," Joe said.

Kim reached across the table. "Here, give me Ami. You two go swimming and I'll make lunch."

Between them they walked Ami across the tabletop and Jenni took the bag containing her bikini inside. Kim looked sideways at Joe, amused at his forced casualness. He stared out over the beach as though something fascinating had drawn his attention. He glanced at her, stood and tugged his shirt over his head, dropped his pants to reveal the tight speedos. He made no effort to hide the bulge his cock made and Kim stared, letting him see her stare, arousal trickling through her.

Jenni returned quickly. She would know the house intimately, having cleaned every corner and crevice over the years. She had probably changed in the downstairs shower room and when she came out Joe stepped down onto the sand below the porch. Kim rose and placed a hand on Jenni's arm, stopping her at the top of the step.

"Don't get in a fight with any more jellies, will you?"

Jenni grinned. "Try not to."

"Good." Kim leaned across and kissed Jenni on the lips, catching Jenni's full bottom lip with her teeth just before she drew back. "Because I've got plans for later."

"Oh?"

Kim slapped Jenni on the ass. "Go on, burn off some energy. We'll eat when you get back."

***

Jenni ran down the steps past Joe, running hard, not knowing if she was running away or toward something. She sensed Joe next to her, and though it was impossible is seemed as though his masculine energy touched her like a warm cocoon. They hit the water and the cold knocked the breath from her and if she had been above the surface she would have laughed. She half expected something to start with Joe while they swam, but he appeared distracted, thinking about something, and they swam out as far as they had the first time and the only indication of what might lie ahead came when he drifted against her, slipped his arms around her back and kissed her hard, once, on the mouth. They sank slowly beneath the swell, sank deep, not touching bottom and Jenni wanted to stay that way forever, locked against Joe, taking her air from him. She knew he was aroused, his cock pressing thick against her thigh, knew she was as well, had been since she rose that morning. They kicked for the surface and without a word Joe rolled and swam away and she stroked hard to catch up.

Coming out from the ocean Jenni was glad she and Joe had gone no further in the water. She would have succumbed, she knew, her willpower sapped by swirling thoughts of sex with both these people. Joe played it cool, treating her exactly as he had every other time and as she splashed from the water she was in control again. This was not going to be about her rolling over and doing anything they wanted, this was going to be about her as well, about what she needed.

Joe fell into step beside her and she glanced at him and grinned. "That was a great swim. Thanks."

"What for?"

"Just thanks."

Joe gave her a puzzled look, Jenni showing him a different person to the one he went into the water with.

As they came into the kitchen Kim was laying four places, Ami already in her highchair with a plastic spoon in her hand, trying to dig something edible from the plastic tray in front of her. Jenni saw Joe stop and then he said, "Solids?"

Kim grinned. "You did say it was time."

"But you... no, great. What's she having?"

"Same as us. Pasta with chicken. Except hers comes out of this cute little jar." Kim held up a small plastic jar with a bright picture printed on the front showing a healthy looking rooster and some twists of frusilli. All business, Kim said, "Joe, you shower upstairs. Jenni you can use the one down here. Ready in ten minutes so don't be long."

Jenni needed only to wash the salt off herself. She closed

the door of the small downstairs shower room and stripped out of her mismatched top and bikini briefs. She shivered with cold once naked, which was stupid, because what she had been wearing made her almost naked anyway. She turned on the electric shower and waited for the heat to start up then stepped under the spray, letting it run through her hair. She shampooed and ran soap over herself quickly, turned so the water cascaded over her head, her hair washing in long ripples down her back.

The door opened and Kim stepped through, still dressed in the flimsy cover-up.

"I brought you the dress, Jen. I thought you might want to wear it today."

"Are you sure?"

"Of course. It looks so much better on you than me. I think Joe likes you in it too."

Kim placed the soft dress on the towel box and stood for a moment staring openly at Jenni.

Jenni was determined not to cover herself, although that was her natural reaction. After what Kim had done to her the week before it seemed ridiculous to pretend, but instinct made her want to lift her hands to her breasts. She saw the way Kim's eyes traced her body. She saw her stiffen, and Jenni realized Kim's sharp gaze had recognized the almost completely faded bruises.

"What are those?" Kim asked, her voice losing all flirtatiousness.

"Nothing," Jenni said, trying to move her arms to cover herself without making it obvious, ashamed to show this woman what Mark had done to her.

Kim stepped across until she was directly in front of her. Water bounced off Jenni's breasts and splashed onto Kim's gauzy covering. Kim was almost in the shower with her, and she lifted Jenni's arm away from her side and bent to look. The bruising had almost disappeared, but a faint dark yellow stain remained beneath her tan.

"Did Mark do this to you?"

Jenni looked to the side. She didn't want to answer.

"Did he?" Kim's voice hard now.

Jenni nodded.

"Does he do this often?"

Jenni shook her head.

"A you telling me the truth, Jen?"

"Every couple of months, maybe. I've gotten used to it." She didn't dare confess that Mark was hitting her more often lately.

"No one should have to get used to this."

"Not everyone's like you and Joe, Kim."

Kim stared at her, so close she was getting almost as wet as Jenni, so close Jenni wanted to kiss her. These two people had unleashed emotions and fantasies inside her she had only rarely entertained since she was a teenager, and never with the strength and inevitability she now felt. Kim turned away, removing the temptation and Jenni was unsure if she was relieved or not.

"Anyway, the dress is there and lunch is on the table. I don't know what Joe is going to say when he sees those."

"Maybe he won't see them," Jenni said.

Kim shot a glance over her shoulder and they both knew Joe was soon going to see everything.

Alone, Jenni lifted her hands to her breasts, not to cover but to lift them. Her thumbs stuck up, the edge of her nails just touching the nipples and finding them erect. Kim would have seen their hardness. Kim would have noticed the nakedness of her labia. She turned the shower off and toweled dry, pulled the jersey dress over her head, stretching her arms high the only way she could squeeze into it, wriggling it down over her curves. God, but it was tight, tighter than the last time. Perhaps washing it had not been such a great idea. She felt more exposed wearing the dress than if she had been naked, but there was nothing else in the room and Jenni knew she didn't care anymore.

She found Kim at the table trying to feed Ami, who had more of the stewed chicken pasta in her hair and over her cheeks than in her mouth.

"She'll get the hang of it," Kim said, trying another spoonful.

"Give her the spoon," Jenni said.

Kim laughed. "Yeah. You want this in your hair too?"

"Try her," Jenni said, sliding into the chair across the table, sitting close to Ami. Ami turned to her and offered a bright smile, the effect rather spoiled by the detritus spattering her sweet face.

Kim opened Ami's fist and placed the spoon inside her palm. Ami looked down and lifted her hand, fascinated by this new toy. Jenni leaned over and led her hand with the spoon to the bowl in front of her, loaded a tiny morsel and then guided Ami's hand back up. Ami stared at Jenni, stared at the spoon, stared at the food then jerked her hand out of Jenni's grip and slapped the spoon against her forehead.

Kim laughed. "Lousy aim."

"She'll get it."

"She might starve first."

Jenni laughed. "You've always got those as backup," nodding at Kim's breasts displayed beneath the cover-up.

"Got what as backup?" Joe asked as he came in, hesitated for a moment then moved round and sat on the same side as Jenni. Jenni noticed Kim flashing him a glance, but it was more amused than annoyed.

"None of your business," Kim said. "Now you've *finally* decided to join us we can eat."

Chapter 15

The food was good but none of them had their mind on eating except for Ami, and even though her mind was on it her co-ordination didn't help and eventually Joe took pity on Jenni and retrieved the spoon, tried to offer what little remained in the bowl. Ami pushed her bottom lip out and her eyes turned watery. Kim picked her up out of the high chair, took her to the sink and washed most of the gunk off before sitting her against her breast. Ami closed her eyes and started to suckle noisily.

The atmosphere grew charged, all of them sensing it. Jenni's head was swimming as if she had finished a bottle of wine, but they had only drunk water. Her fingers tingled with the need to touch someone, to touch skin, to touch secret, sensitive places only a lover knows. Her breath caught in her chest and she knew the skin tight jersey was telegraphing her arousal to Kim and Joe, her nipples straining against the sheer material and she didn't dare glance down.

Joe was talking about something, explaining how he was going to need to go on a book tour when they returned to New York, how he hated them but knew they was an essential evil, and Jenni heard herself asking perfectly logical and sane questions but it sounded as though they came from far away and from someone else.

"... London, Paris, Amsterdam, Copenhagen, down to Milan and Rome, over to Madrid, back to England for the Oxford Literary Festival then this really tiny town called Hay on Wye where they've turned the whole place over to books. I'll be gone a couple of months."

Jenni listened to his answer but had forgotten the original question; all she heard was his voice, dark and rich, the rumble it made in the air, the resonance is caused in her chest.

"Will Kim and Ami go with you?"

Joe shook his head. "Kim hates all the false sycophancy and

hypocrisy. I'll try and get back if I get a chance, but we both know I've got to do the tour. It's only every couple of years." Joe stared into her eyes, seemed about to add something before thinking better of it.

Across the table Kim pulled Ami from her nipple and lifted her to her shoulder. Rub... circle... rub... loud expulsion of gas. Ami's breathing changed, grew soft and sibilant. Kim stood and handed Ami's soft, boneless body to Joe who took her upstairs to her cot.

Jenni started clearing the table, stacking dishes, running water into the sink.

"We can leave these," Kim said, standing behind her, standing so close Jenni felt the heat radiating from her.

"It won't take long to do them now."

"I usually take a nap after lunch. Why don't you do the same?"

Kim was offering something else but Jenni still found herself saying, "I've never done that."

"There's always a first time for everything," Kim said, her hands touching Jenni's hips and lingering. Joe came back and looked at them.

"Shall I stack?"

"Jenni insists on washing the dishes now," Kim said. She leaned her cheek against Jenni's shoulder, her breasts pressed to Jenni's back.

"I'll dry and you stack. Five minutes and we'll be done."

Jenni swirled water around the plates, handed them to Joe. Joe dried and placed them on the worktop. Kim picked them up and stacked them in the cupboards. They had managed to half finish before Kim gave a strangled moan and came back to stand behind Jenni. Her hands slid around Jenni's hips and without thinking Jenni leaned back into the embrace. It was an instant of abandon and suddenly everything tipped beyond control. Kim's hands lifted from Jenni's hips and circled her stomach, rose again and cupped the deep undercurve of her breasts. The sensation of having another woman holding her breasts forced a sound from deep inside Jenni's throat. Her head was spinning. She had her hands still buried in hot water but barely noticed.

Joe moved close against Jenni's side and touched her face with soft fingers, turning her toward him, and as she came around his lips met hers and the contact sent shivers through her core.

Kim dropped her hands again and Jenni wanted Joe to touch her breasts now but he waited. Kim lowered her hands to the hem of the tight dress and tugged, easing the stretch material upward. Jenni offered no resistance, cool air touching her thighs as the dress rose, allowing herself to be revealed, wanting to be revealed, the air touching her shaved labia, touching her hips. The dress gathered at her waist and Kim went to her knees and kissed Jenni on the small of her back, started to kiss around the edge of her ass, moving lower all the time and Jenni recalled Kim's tongue against her ass and almost swooned. They were both touching her, Joe kissing her arched neck and Jenni closed her eyes, losing herself in the sensation of two people caressing her body. She wanted this, believed she had wanted this forever, but unsure until this moment. Yes! She wanted this.

Joe's hand touched her belly bared by the dress and started working higher. The undersides of her breasts became exposed as he drew the dress upward and now Joe did touch her, stroking his fingers along the full curves, pulling, lifting the dress over her breasts until they swung free and the dress was around her neck, her arms still encased in a second skin but the rest of her body naked. Joe bent and sucked a rigid nipple between his lips, bit gently with his teeth and Jenni's knees buckled. Kim had reached the back of her thighs and worked her way around to the front. Joe shifted, replacing her, standing behind Jenni and cupping her breasts in his hands. Jenni's breasts spilled over the side of Joe's hands. She leaned back into him, grinding herself against the hardness pressing into the small of her back. Kim moved around and kissed Jenni's stomach, tasting her skin with tiny, teasing pecks. Jenni was awash with lust, abandoned by sense or shame. These two could do with her as they wished, anything they wished; Jenni wanted everything, wanted to abandon herself to their will. She dropped her hand behind to Joe's pants, the long ridge formed by his cock beneath her fingers. Joe pressed himself into her touch, moving so his covered cock slid against her hand.

Kim pushed Jenni backward, trying to open her thighs for her tongue and Jenni allowed access, leaning against Joe who moved back and knocked into a chair. The legs scraped against the wooden floor and Joe sat abruptly, pulling Jenni against him, lifting her hair and placing his mouth against her neck. Jenni moaned and touched her breast, the rigid tip of her nipple, having never known it as hard and sensitive as now. Kim's tongue found her clitoris as she scuttled forward between Jenni's legs.

Jenni fumbled beneath herself with Joe's pants, struggling to free his cock and he dropped his hands, his mouth remaining clamped to her neck, and helped, unzipping and pushing his pants down and suddenly Jenni's fingers were around the hot bare skin of his cock and she gripped him, so much thicker and longer than Mark. Kim's tongue worked against her hard. Joe's naked legs and cock pressed against her ass and Jenni rubbed him frantically, her closed fist striking Kim as she sucked at Jenni's clitoris. The tremor started deep back inside her belly and Jenni knew she was going to come harder than she ever had in her life. She whimpered as she felt the orgasm build and blossom. Jenni twisted away from Kim's tongue, towards Joe, lifting her legs and straddling him so his cock pressed against her belly, dropped her head to Joe's neck and bit him, not caring if she left a mark. Jenni jerked and Kim came back at her from behind, her mouth exploring her back, her ass parted as she leaned toward Joe and Kim's tongue found her as it had found her last week, touched the nestled bud and Jenni cried out against Joe's neck as her knees shook. All sensation left her legs as her being centered between her thighs, the rush and explosion too much to bear and Jenni's conscious mind swirled and departed, the whole world graying out and fading.

She didn't think she passed out, not quite, because when she next became aware she was still upright on Joe's lap. Kim had slipped her hand beneath Jenni, freeing Joe's cock and she sucked him, her head bumping against Jenni's ass. Jenni climbed off Joe, stood breathing hard watching Kim fellate her husband.

She knelt behind Kim, kissing her shoulder. Kim was still dressed in bikini bottoms and the thin cover-up and Jenni pushed the top aside, slipping her hands inside to grasp Kim's small, neat breasts. Kim shivered as Jenni's fingers found her sensitive nipples.

Joe pushed Kim away and stood, breathing hard.

"I want to take you upstairs," he said. "Both of you."

Jenni looked up at him past Kim's head. Joe stood unashamed, his hard cock pulsing with each heartbeat. Jenni tried to reach around Kim and kiss his gorgeous cock but was unable to reach. Kim moved beneath her, also rising.

"I want that too," she said.

Jenni looked at them, still on her knees. She could reach Joe's cock now but was suddenly shy. This was the moment, the one she had dreamed of since she had first seen this perfect couple. She nodded and offered her hand.

***

The bedroom window was open and a breeze caught at the light drapes, billowing them into the room. The surf sounded loud, the tide bringing it close. Joe had left his pants on the kitchen floor, pulled his t-shirt off and lay on his back on the bed, hands behind his head, a smile on his handsome face.

Kim removed the cover-up, stripped her bikini briefs off. She turned to Jenni and tugged the ridiculous, wonderful jersey dress over her head, took Jenni's hand and led her to the bed. There was no sense of oddness, what they were doing seemed the most natural thing in the world. Jenni wanted this, wanted this like she had never wanted anything before.

Jenni knelt on the edge of the bed and leaned over Joe, gripping his cock, finally doing what she had wanted to do since revealing him. She dipped and kissed the smooth head. It was slick with Joe's pre-cum and Jenni closed her full lips around the base of his glans and let her tongue slip and probe against the oozing opening. She heard Joe gasp. Kim's head rested against hers. Kim pushed against her, licking Joe's shaved balls heavy with promise. Jenni wanted him completely. She took him deeper into her mouth, gripping his shaft tight within her lips, wetting half his length. She needed more. Mark had not let her take his cock in her mouth for years, had never wanted her to do this thing she loved. Jenni remembered the last time someone had come in her mouth, is seemed so long ago, and she reached down to touch herself and found her pussy slick and sensitive. She pushed down on Joe, wanting all of him, the head of his cock bumping against the back of her mouth. Jenni opened her lips wider and pressed harder, letting the top of Joe's cock slide into her throat. She breathed hard through her nose, experiencing no reflex to gag, she never had, only fulfillment.

"Oh my God!" Jenni heard Kim gasp next to her. "How in hell can you do that?"

Jenni couldn't answer, didn't want to answer, wanted only the wonderful sensation of Joe's cock filling her mouth. She began to move against him, bobbing rapidly, wanting him to lose control. She saw Kim move again, glimpsed as she slid down the bed out of sight, then felt Kim once more nestle down behind and start to kiss her ass, her tongue darting out onto Jenni's asshole. The girl was obsessed, Jenni thought, but it felt so damn good she didn't care. It seemed as though nothing was out of bounds today... and tomorrow, and the days after that, she could not wait to see what those days brought.

She pulled back until just the very tip of Joe's cock rested against her lips. Her hand found his shaft, slippery with her own saliva. She dipped again, taking him in one smooth motion all the way inside, pushing her lips down against short pubic hair. She repeated the motion, lifting so he barely touched her lips, drew him in, over and over, aware of Joe growing ever harder inside her mouth. She cradled his balls as they tightened and pulled close. She loved the sense of power in her mouth and body, knowing she possessed a control over both these people. She had not experienced these feelings for so long and reveled in them, reveled in the pleasure she was capable of giving another person.

Joe twisted his fingers into her long hair and it hurt but she didn't care. He urged her down, ready to commit. Jenni teased with her lips and tongue. Joe's grip became more forceful. She relented, taking him deep into her throat. Joe jerked suddenly and a gush of hot semen exploded in her mouth and Jenni swallowed hard. Joe erupted again, filling her mouth before she was ready and Jenni knew his cum was dripping from her lips and loved the idea they would both see that. The sensation of him emptying into her mouth sent her over, Kim licking her ass and fingering her clitoris helped and her body responded, shaking and twitching as she came for the second time in quick succession. She had rarely done that before, rarely experienced a second climax so soon after the first. Joe pushed into her mouth, still emptying, his semen coating her cheeks and mouth, trailing along her chin and neck.

Kim darted back up, pushed Jenni on her back and kissed her mouth. Jenni had no choice but to respond, no other decision offered and Kim's tongue came into her mouth and she found she was kissing back before she realized what was happening. She slumped backward, reveling in the tease of another woman's breasts against her own, and then Joe was rolling over, still hard. His cock pressed against the closed slit of her pussy and Jenni spread her legs wide, wanting him, wanting it all. She felt Joe's weight settle against her, felt his hips slide along her thighs, widening her further, his cock opened her slit and entered, the movement steady and fast until Joe was buried deep inside her. Jenni gave a purr far back in her throat and heard Kim laugh at her reaction.

"He's good, isn't he?" Kim whispered against her mouth.

Jenni nodded. "He feels so good. So big."

"Mm, I like it," Kim said, twisting to watch. "I like watching Joe fuck you, watching his cock inside your pussy." Kim kissed Jenni's breasts. "You are so beautiful, baby."

Joe leaned down and kissed the other breast. Kim and Joe lifted their heads and kissed each other. A sound escaped Jenni as she watched their mouths work against each other directly in front of her. This could not be happening to her, but it was, the reality of her sensations swamping her. Joe whispered something into Kim's ear and she grinned. Joe tugged Jenni hard, moving her down the bed and Kim's breasts slid against her. Jenni reached with her lips, found a nipple and licked it. The sweet taste of milk ran across her tongue and Jenni lifted her head and took the nipple deep into her mouth, sucking hard, moaning as Kim's milk spurted against her tongue.

Kim pulled away and Joe's mouth replaced Jenni's. Jenni saw Kim's milk trail down Joe's chin when he sat back. All the time he continued the solid pumping inside her and Jenni pushed against him, astounded at how good the sensation was, regretting all the years of accepting what she had when something as strong as this existed in the world. Kim sat up and kissed Joe, pressing against him. The move raised her body and she lifted a leg and straddled Jenni's waist, pushing her pussy against Joe's belly. Jenni gripped Kim's waist in her hands, such a tiny waist. She ran her hands down over Kim's ass, slim and pert. A moment's hesitation stopped her before she laughed softly and slipped her fingers between Kim's legs to find her pussy wet and welcoming.

Kim arched her back, pressing down on Jenni's fingers. Kim leaned against Joe and inch by inch moved her ass back along Jenni's body. As Kim moved backward Jenni dipped her fingers deeper inside. Kim's leg brushed her chin. She turned and kissed insider her thigh. Kim came further back and Jenni was flooded with the realization of what Kim wanted, flooded with the realization she wanted it too. Jenni gripped Kim's hips and pulled her back, extending her tongue as Kim's pussy settled against her mouth. Another first. Another wonderful first. Jenni tasted the nectar of Kim's pussy, tasted another woman for the very first time and wondered why she had denied herself this for so long. There had been girls in High School, and afterwards; women who let it be known they wanted her. Jenni was aware many people wanted her, but even though it was a fact of her life she never translated that want into a sense of self-worth. She searched inside Kim with her tongue, discovering her taste, the sensation of another woman against her mouth unbelievable. She shifted focus and moved back and up, to the place obsessing Kim. Jenni was beyond restraint, beyond disgust. She circled Kim's tiny pink asshole with her tongue, touched the center. For a brief moment she waited, tasting the other woman, waiting for something to stop her but nothing did, and she made her tongue hard and pushed against the tight ring.

Kim's hand came down against her breasts, pulling and kneading them, almost painful but wonderful. Jenni reached around and found Kim's clitoris and rubbed it hard as Kim worked against her tongue. Kim was gasping, starting to shake, and Jenni realized she was making this happen. The knowledge she was capable of doing this to the gorgeous Kim filled her beyond capacity and she knew she was going to come as well, allowing herself to peak at the same time so they both jerked and shook against each other.

Jenni heard Joe's breathing quicken as he watched them both quake with pleasure. He pulled out of her as Kim slumped backward. Joe moved fast, straddling Jenni's waist. He rubbed himself hard but Jenni half sat and pushed his hand aside, replacing it with her own. She wanted to be the one making him come. Joe groaned and curled over. Jenni rubbed fast, looking down at him as the first jet splashed across her breasts, then another and Joe twitched and gasped. Jenni stroked him until he pulled away, growing sensitive. Jenni spread his semen over her breasts, lost in abandoned sensation.

Joe rolled aside and came back to cradle her against him. Kim moved to her other side. Their hands touched her body, her face and neck and breasts and belly, sliding through the slippery semen that covered her, sliding through the sweat that coated them all. Kim tilted Jenni's chin in her fingers and kissed her, then Joe tilted her the other way and repeated the offering.

"I hope you don't mind getting messy," Joe said. "I wasn't sure if you were using any birth control, and I thought..." He took the crumpled sheet and starting wiping away the trails of semen he had deposited across her. He used the sheets to wipe her clean, working away until she was dry.

Joe's tenderness made Jenni choke up inside, but she forced a laugh. "I liked getting messy, Joe. And I'm on the pill, but it would have been okay anyway." A thrill ran through her as she thought of Joe filling her with his cum. Of his seed merging with hers and a life growing inside her belly. A wave of sadness rolled through Jenni as she realized what she had been suppressing all these years. Yes, she wanted a baby, more than one, but Mark was never going to give in. She felt tears well in her eyes. Oh God, what was she going to do? Here in this sun washed bedroom was not real; back home in her tiny house reality lay and she would have to return there.

"Hey babe," Kim sat up, touching the tears tracking along Jenni's cheek. "We didn't mean to upset you."

Jenni shook her head. "It's not you. It's me. My fucking shit life, that's what this is all about."

Joe looked at Kim across her body, looked back. "You can change your life, if you want."

Jenni laughed through the hitching in her chest. "Yeah, and Pinocchio's going to turn into a real boy."

Kim kissed her cheek. "You can do anything you want, Jenni. This is your life... come with us, if that's what you want."

Jenni heard her words but didn't hear them.

"What am I going to do? I..." She stopped suddenly, afraid of what she had been about to say. She was incapable of uttering those words, not now, not yet; maybe never.

"We want you," Kim said, her face close to Jenni's. "If you want it too, you can have this, Jenni, have this all the time. We both want you to come home with us."

This time Jenni heard and she rolled her head to look at Kim. A spark of hope flared in her breast, but she doused the emotion. "Why?" she asked, her voice colder than she meant.

"Because we love you," Kim said.

Jenni looked across at Joe. He continued stroking her breasts, fascinated, but he was watching the exchange between Jenni and his wife.

"How can you love me," Jenni said, still holding herself back. "You hardly know me. You only met me two weeks ago."

"Time means nothing to the heart," Kim said. "We both know how we feel about you."

Jenni glanced back at Joe. "What about you?" she asked. "Do you think the same way?"

He nodded, looking into her eyes. "We have never met anyone like you, Jenni. We want you to come and live with us."

Jenni laughed, a harsh bark. "Fuck!" she exhaled. "I'm not some fucking sex toy!"

"Jenni," Kim said, and Jenni heard tears in her voice too. "We don't want you for that. Well, not just for that, because I do want sex with you, lots and lots of sex, you and me, you and Joe, me and Joe, all of us together. I want that. We both want that. But only if you do too. More than anything else we want to set you free, to let you be the woman we know you are, the woman we know you can be."

Jenni watched Kim struggling to say what she needed, but it still seemed wrong to her.

"You can't stay here," Joe said, his voice soft and reasonable and Jenni turned on her side to face him. His hand rested on her hip and Kim pressed against her from behind. "We love you because you're strong, Jen. You've hit us both hard. Nothing like this has ever happened before, and this is as tough on us as I can see it is for you. That doesn't mean it's wrong, babe. We want you so much... but we know it's your decision, and we'll respect whatever decision you make."

Jenni looked at him as she lay sandwiched between man and wife. Conflicting emotions warred inside her. She wanted to accept their offer, wanted to lie like this between them forever, make love to both, watch Ami grow into a woman. Another side was afraid, feared the change and the danger, a small part of her believing she didn't deserve happiness. She feared these two may only be playing with her and would discard her when they grew tired of their toy.

She shook her head, trying to rattle the confusion out. From the other room they heard a cry as Ami woke. Kim rolled away and padded through. The crying stopped.

"I don't know how I can say this," Joe said, "not without it sounding strange and creepy, but I love you, Jenni, and Kim loves you too."

Kim came back into the room, Ami on her hip, happy now.

"Ami loves you as well," Kim said, and laid her daughter down on Jenni's naked belly. Ami squirmed happily and Jenni put her arms around the tiny body and held her against her as more tears flowed, but these were not the same tears as before. These were tears of joy.

Chapter 16

Kim smiled looking through the kitchen window, watching as Joe and Jenni walked down the beach to the breakers. They were comfortable, relaxed with each other. Jenni said something to make Joe laugh and Kim felt something turn over inside her, something good. No room existed in her heart for jealousy. Jenni might make the break and come to New York with them, she might not. Whatever the decision, Kim felt secure with Joe. Even though the situation was new to them both, she held a conviction her relationship with Joe had permanence. Kim smiled, wondering where her obsession with sex had come from. Before Ami, before the pregnancy, she and Joe enjoyed a good sex life but it had never been spectacular, more lukewarm than hot. Since Ami arrived Kim sensed a change inside herself, and so far the change seemed permanent. She had never looked at another woman before with anything other than friendship. Only four months into her pregnancy she discovered herself wondering how old friends might look naked. She made no move to act on these thoughts, but both she and Joe benefited from the new awakening inside her. Now, with this wonderful woman who had, almost literally, washed up on their doorstep, the world was tilting on its axis.

Joe and Jenni reached the breakers and pushed through. Kim shaded her eyes until she lost sight of them among the swell, turned back to finish preparing dinner. Ami was sitting on the floor, her nappy-padded bottom tilting her forward and every now and again she waved her legs and arms and scooted across the slick wooden floor, making incoherent words that meant something only to her.

***

As Joe reached the water he turned back and waved, not sure if Kim remained at the window or not. Sun reflected off glass hiding the evidence of anyone standing on the other side. He turned back to the ocean, heavy waves washing against him and he grinned, enjoying the way Jenni's body slipped through the water, the way muscle moved beneath her skin. He did not see the big shiny pickup parked on the road behind their house, pulled up on the side of the track. Even if he had seen he would have suspected nothing. Kids were always driving down to the beach to make out or park and go surfing.

***

Mark Adams sat in the cab of his pickup and lit a new cigarette from the butt of the old. A pint bottle of cheap bourbon rested uncapped on the seat beside him. The distant figures of his wife and the city guy moved through the surf and started to swim beyond the breakers. Dead man walking, Mark thought, and chuckled to himself. That bitch wife of his too. Mark's own bitch wife as well, he supposed. All had to go. They couldn't treat him like this. He knew exactly what was going on, and whatever happened next was down to them, not him. Rich city slickers coming to *his* town, playing around with *his* wife. No one would blame him. Hell, he deserved a medal.

He should be on his way to meet the guys now, and he experienced a moment's regret. Couldn't be avoided. He had more important business to take care of here.

He straightened and flicked his cigarette through the window. Okay. Decision made. The bitch first. The baby next, he guessed, though he experienced a brief moment of guilt the baby would have to go. Maybe not the baby. Mark leaned his head back against the seat, his surge of energy draining away, and closed his eyes. He was suddenly bone weary. How was a man supposed to sleep when his wife was fucking complete strangers? How many times had she done this before and he hadn't known? Perhaps he'd rest up for a minute, get his strength back; not that he was going to need much strength for these city folk. He sucked on a new cigarette, moved his head so it rested in the angle between seat and door. He heard surf pounding against the sand, a sound he heard most nights of his life as he lay awake into the small hours, trying to damp down the anger burning in his gut.

***

Kim finished cubing beef and chopping vegetables, placed everything in one large pot and turned the oven on low. The stew could sit as long as needed now. Ami would need another feed in an hour, and Jenni and Joe would be back by then. If Ami went down after her feed, Kim wanted to go back upstairs. She had unfinished business, an ache in her loins she felt might never be satisfied.

Kim stared at the oven, a small frown troubling her brow. She wanted to make something for after dinner. Pancakes, maybe? Yeah, pancakes sounded good. She had seen a big cast iron griddle that went over the gas ring somewhere and she searched through the cabinets until she found it, struggling to lift it down, gripping the handles on both sides, the round metal circle thick and heavy. She laid it carefully on the worktop and mixed up some batter, lay a cover over and left it to stand.

She sat cross legged on the floor in front of Ami and when the child reached out to her gripped her fists and pulled her to her feet. Ami grinned as though she had accomplished the cleverest trick in the world. She had been making a lot of noises lately, meaningless grunts and cries, and even though Kim knew it was way too early she liked to think Ami was trying to communicate.

She pulled over a small pile of blocks, each one three inches on a side, each face showing a different letter of the alphabet alternating with an animal starting with the letter. The one she held had G printed large on one face, smaller on the remaining three, together with a drawing of a Giraffe, a Goat and a Gorilla. Kim held the block inside her hands, Ami waiting with anticipation because she knew this game. It didn't matter how many times they played, the unmasking always came as a complete surprise to the infant.

Kim moved her hands closer and Ami wriggled in anticipation.

"Gorilla!" Kim said quickly, revealing the silverback. Ami squealed loudly, laughing so hard she tumbled backwards and bumped her head on the floor. The laughter turned instantly to tears, ending almost as quickly as Kim righted her and unmasked... *Giraffe*!

She didn't hear the back door open, the one facing away from the sea, the one they never used and always forgot to lock. Only when Ami looked up past her did she realize someone had entered the kitchen. She span around on the slick floor to discover Jenni's husband standing in the doorway.

***

The bitch sat on the floor, not even aware he had entered the room until the brat gave him away. Mark watched her turn and start to rise to her feet. Her tits spilled from her open shirt as she leaned over and Mark watched them, sudden arousal taking him by surprise. Maybe dispatching her could wait a minute or two.

"What do you want?" she asked.

Mark grinned. "Put the baby somewhere."

"What are you doing here!" Kim put herself between him and the child.

"Nothing. To her. Put her away, now, before I change my mind."

"No." Kim paled, but her face set in a determined frown.

Mark leaned against the worktop, running his hand across the smooth wood. This was one nice house. He wondered how much a place like this cost to rent. More than he made in a month, he bet.

"I don't think you understand." He spoke as though she was the child. "If you don't put her away, I'll do her first and make you watch. Now, put the fucking baby somewhere and shut the fuck up." He was suddenly breathing hard and made an effort to calm himself. She only needed to do as he asked and this would go easier on all of them.

"You have to promise you won't touch her."

"I promise," Mark said. If Kim knew him better she would have realized he never kept his word, but he saw the fear for her baby overarching everything in her mind. She leaned over and picked Ami up. The infant started crying, not knowing what was happening, but responding to the atmosphere in the room. Kim carried her past Mark and put a foot on the stair.

"Not upstairs," Mark said.

"Her cot's upstairs." Kim took the second step, then the third.

Mark watched her go. His hand moved, barely aware he was picking up the long Sabatier from the wooden block before he followed.

***

Kim expected him to pull her back but she reached the landing, laid Ami in her cot in the back room. She turned quickly, intending to climb out on the balcony and see if she could jump down to the beach, but Mark had followed her closely, bringing the long Sabatier with him, ten inches of gleaming steel. Kim recalled Joe sharpening the blade only that morning. Why did he have to love those damn knives so much?

"Thinking of going somewhere?" Mark asked.

Kim shook her head, afraid now, more afraid than she had been downstairs. It was different up here, their territory, her and Joe's, the sense of invasion stronger.

Mark looked beyond her, through the doorway into the bedroom. He nodded at the door. "In there."

Kim backed away and he followed, the knife held loose at his side.

Mark kicked the door closed behind him and Kim came to a halt with her legs against the foot of the bed.

"Strip."

"What?"

"Take 'em all off. Not that you got much to take off, but I want it all off. Now!"

"Fuck you."

He closed the gap in an instant, the wicked blade coming up and resting against her cheek. "There's something you need to understand here sweetheart. I'm the one in charge, and what I say goes. So strip."

Kim knew she was crying but was incapable of stopping. Mark stepped away, not far enough to allow her any chance of escape but far enough she couldn't reach him. Kim pulled her open shirt off and let it drop to the floor. Mark's eyes tracked down her body, came back up as she reached around and pulled the tie on her bikini top. She dropped it next to her blouse.

Mark waved the knife. "Those too, honey."

Kim bit her lip and bent over, stripping her bikini briefs down, stood naked in front of him.

"Fuckin' slut," he said, staring at her shaved pussy. He started to fumble with his jeans. He was unable to undo them one handed so shuffled across to the dressing table and put the knife down. He caught Kim's glance and shook his head. "You can try if you like. Make it a little more fun. Come on, darlin', give it a try..."

Now his hands were free he unhooked his belt and tugged at the zip of his jeans. He pulled them down, then his shorts and stood with his erection jutting out.

"You wanna come lie down and deal with this first? Before we conclude our piece of business?"

"Why would I do that? If you're going to kill me do it, but I'd rather burn in hell than have you anywhere near me."

Mark shrugged. "Suit yourself." He picked up the knife again. He shuffled across, looking ridiculous with his jeans around his ankles, and if not for the gleaming knife Kim would have laughed.

As Mark reached her Kim moved backward away from him. The bed caught behind her knees and she swayed. Mark reached for her breast and she leaned back further, suddenly falling onto the bed. Mark landed on top of her, forcing air from her lungs, and for a moment she didn't know if he had used the knife or not, then she saw it beside her on the bed. Mark tried to force her knees apart, his stupid tiny prick pressing against her. He stank of bourbon and cigarettes and stale sweat and automotive grease, and Kim felt something break loose inside and kicked up between his legs, her knee finding a target. Mark grunted but stayed on top of her. He lifted the knife and lay it cold against her neck, its razor edge touching her skin, and she felt a welling of blood.

"Now, we can do this with you moving or not, sweetheart.

So which is it going to be?"

Kim wanted to spit in his face, stopped herself. He meant it. He was too far gone to care whether he fucked her alive or dead, and alive she would maybe get another chance. She turned her head to one side as he tried to kiss her, pulling the knife away, but he wasn't gentle and Kim felt it slice into her flesh once again and more blood flowed. Great, she thought, now he kills me by accident.

"Open wide," Mark said, and Kim parted her knees and let him drop down between her legs.

"Come on. At least it's not going to take long."

Mark chuckled. "Feisty, ain't we?" He probed around, trying to find her entrance. "We'll see how feisty you are in a minute, sweet tits. I bet you like this, don't you? Like a real man for a change. Okay, sweetheart, let's see how you like these apples."

Kim knew when he found her entrance at last. She squeezed her eyes tight shut, tried to ignore the wail coming from Ami's room. Mark didn't seem to hear it at all, but Kim's instinct responded to the cries of her daughter and her nipples spurted milk, sudden and automatic.

"Oh fuck, that's gross!" Mark groaned and pulled away. "Shit no, what the fuck are you doing?"

"Nothing. This is natural, but you wouldn't recognize natural would you."

"Oh fuck," Mark said again. He was sitting back from her, still hard, his face a mask of disgust. He shook his head. "No way, man. No way."

Kim saw his face change, going from disgust to something dreamy. He picked up the knife and laid it against his own cheek and smiled.

"Ah well, guess I'll have to fuck Jenni instead."

He leaned forward, bringing the knife around just as the bedroom door flew open and Joe said, "Get off her, cunt."

Mark swung around, the knife catching Kim under her left breast and opening the skin. Mark laughed. "Come on in and watch, faggot, see how a real man works."

"Okay," Joe said, and closed the five paces between the

door and the bed, moving fast and without hesitation. He grabbed Mark by his hair and tugged his head back. Beyond him Kim saw Jenni enter the bedroom, holding another knife, one of the smaller ones.

Joe pulled harder and Mark screamed. Joe punched him on the ribcage and then stopped, making an odd grunting sound.

Kim looked down and screamed. The Sabatier was embedded in Joe's shoulder, in the soft part just below his clavicle, embedded deeply and blood was starting to well around the blade.

Mark laughed. "Fuck you."

Joe staggered back as Mark stood, bending over and pulling his jeans up, his eyes never leaving Jenni.

"I hope he was worth it," he sneered.

"He is," Jenni said. "And so is Kim."

Mark snarled and lunged at her but Jenni darted to one side, the knife held in front of her. Mark might be drunk but he was judging the situation as well as anyone. He glared at all three of them, looked in satisfaction as Joe leaned against the wall and began to slide down it. Mark darted out through the door.

Kim rushed across to Joe and put her hand beside the knife lodged in his flesh.

"I'm okay," Joe said between gritted teeth. "Hurts like all hell, but I'll live. Go after him, Kim," he said.

Kim hesitated, looking into his face, turned and nodded at Jenni. "Come on, let's finish this."

Jenni nodded back and followed her, leaving wet footprints beside Joe's on the dry wooden floor. Kim didn't glance back or she would have seen Joe's head rock as the world span around him and he sank sideways onto the floor.

***

Kim's stomach turned over as Ami's cries escalated to an all out wail. She dashed downstairs where the noise was coming from and into the kitchen. Mark was standing in the middle of the floor. He had found another knife. For God's sake, Kim thought, why does this house have so *many* fucking knives? Ami dangled loosely from Mark's hand, his fingers gripping her around the arm. She screamed constantly, the sound filling the room, cutting into Kim's head.

Jenni passed her, going straight for Mark, her smaller knife extended.

"Put the baby down!"

Mark grinned. "Gonna make me, sweetheart?"

"If I have to."

Mark nodded. "Maybe I'd like that. Show me a little emotion for once. Come on then." He waved the knife at her.

Mark's eyes were locked on Jenni, on the knife she held in front of her. It was such an obviously uneven contest there could only be one victor, and both Jenni and Mark knew it, but Kim realized Jenni didn't care. She was ready and willing to lay her life down for them. She advanced on Mark.

Ignored, Kim moved to one side and reached out blindly on the worktop. Her hand closed around the handle of the heavy skillet she had put out for pancakes. She pulled it closer, added a second hand. The skillet was large, forged from cast-iron and she needed both hands to lift it.

Mark let go of Ami, tossing her aside like an empty beer can. She hit the floor and skidded, stopped when she came up against the leg of the table. She lay on her side, face crimson, her cries scorching the air.

Jenni advanced more quickly toward Mark.

"No!" Kim shouted, stopping Jenni in her tracks.

Mark turned to her, suddenly aware a second woman was in the room, the one he had dismissed as harmless. Kim swung the skillet two handed, momentum building in her. It was too heavy for her, but she found strength from somewhere and Mark turned fully toward her, not believing what he saw. He started to lift his hand holding the knife just as the skillet caught him square between the eyes. The thwack of cast iron on bone for a moment overwhelmed even Ami's screams. There was a hush. Kim heard the knife drop from Mark's fingers and clatter on the floor. A second later Mark's body thumped dully on the wood. He lay still. No blood flowed but a dark bruise spread instantly between his eyes. Both women watched as his legs spasmed once and fell still.

Kim realized she was standing completely naked, the skillet still in her hand. She dropped it and went across to Ami, picked her up and comforted her. Jenni knelt beside Mark, placed her fingers against his neck. Kim watched as she moved her fingers, searching for a pulse.

"Have I..." Kim failed to finish the sentence.

"He's dead," Jenni said, confirming the obvious.

"What am I... Oh my God, Jenni, what am I going to do?"

Jenni sat back on her heels and looked at Kim. "Nothing. You're going to look after Kim and Joe. I'll take care of this."

"Take care of what?" They both turned at Joe's strained voice. He swayed and leaned against the door and Kim went to him, took his arm and led him to a chair. He sat heavily and then stared at Mark's body as though it was not registering on him.

"I killed him," Kim said matter of factly, kneeling in front of her husband. Jenni came across and took Ami from her, continued the comforting and slowly the infant stopped screaming and subsided into hitching sobs.

Kim looked at the body, not really taking in what had happened.

"You have to take this knife out of me," Joe said.

"We've got to take you to the hospital."

Joe shook his head. "What about him?"

"I think the hospital's too late for him," Kim said.

"We can't go to the emergency room," Jenni said. "They're going to want to know how Joe got a knife in his chest, and then they'll want to know everything, and they'll find out about Mark and...and..." She started crying and Ami, sensing her pain, decided to join in.

"Ah, fuck it!" Joe said. He gripped the black wooden handle of the knife and pulled hard. "Shit!" He screamed, but the blade came free and the knife dropped from his fingers. Fresh blood welled up and ran down his chest. A lot of blood.

"Towels," Jenni said, taking control, and Kim ran to the sink and brought back drying cloths and hand towels. She pressed hard against Joe's wound, trying to stem the outpouring.

Jenni placed Ami back on the floor, ignoring her renewed

cries, and went to the freezer. She cracked ice and poured it into a plastic bag, brought it back and pressed it against Joe, who groaned loudly. Blood now covered half his chest and was running down over his belly. It dripped from his thighs to the floor.

"I think I've ruined these speedos," he said, in a perfectly rational voice.

"How much blood is that?" Kim asked, her eyes wide as she took in the widening pool.

"Not enough to kill him. Not yet," Jenni said. She lifted the towels from Joe and peered beneath. "Get more, Kim."

Kim went to the laundry room and brought back the big white towels Jenni had fetched that morning, still wrapped in plastic. She split them and ran water over each towel in the sink, took them back and Jenni tossed the soaked ones aside and pressed the new towels against Joe's wound. As Jenni revealed the gash, Kim watched in horror as fresh blood gathered and ran out.

"It's okay. I think it's stopping," Jenni said. "What about you?"

Kim glanced down at herself, aware for the first time that blood streaked her belly from the cut beneath her breast. The wound had stopped bleeding, the blood drying.

"I'm fine. But we've got to take Joe to the ER."

"Not yet. Give it five minutes. If he's no better we'll take him, but remember, Kim, it was me hit Mark, not you."

Kim shook her head. "No. I hit him." Her mind was confused, but she recalled that clearly.

"You didn't. Did you see her hit him, Joe?"

"I didn't see anything," Joe said.

"You did. You saw *me* hit Mark with the skillet," Jenni said firmly.

"Fuck, it hurts," Joe said.

"Good," Jenni said. "That means you're alive."

"Ha ha ha," Joe said, slowly and deliberately.

Jenni pulled the towel away from his shoulder. Kim felt relief flood her. The bleeding was definitely slowing, the towel not completely soaked like the first had been. Jenni leaned forward to examine the wound, watching fresh blood well up and run down Joe's chest. She nodded as though satisfied.

"He's still bleeding," Kim said. "I'm calling an ambulance."

"No!" Both Jenni and Joe spoke together. Jenni said. "Have you got a first aid kit?"

"First aid kit?" Kim said, not sure a first aid kit was enough for this. "We brought Ami with us. Fuck, Jen, we got enough medical supplies to service a small war." She turned away and came back after a minute with a large plastic box.

Jenni rummaged through the contents, pulled out gauze and padding and wide strips of plaster. She lifted the towel from Joe again.

"Okay, this is going to hurt some," she said.

Joe nodded. "Just be quick."

"You know me so well already," Jenni joked.

Joe shook his head. "Bad timing, honey."

"Okay. Sorry." She wiped as much of the dried blood as possible from around the wound, pressed a gauze bandage against his shoulder then wrapped more bandage under his arm and back around his shoulder. She tore strips from the roll of plaster and stuck it all down.

"Try and stand," she said. "Lean on me and see if you can stand up."

Joe put his arm on her shoulder and let her take most of the weight as he stood.

"Dizzy?" Jenni asked.

"Some."

"Gonna pass out?"

Joe shook his head. "Don't think so."

"Good. Sit down again."

Joe did as he was told and Jenni pulled a chair across. She sat and leaned her elbows on her knees, stared down at the dead body of her husband. Watching her Kim thought perhaps that ought to be ex-husband and giggled, some part of her knowing she was hysterical but unable to stop herself. She needed to be busy. She opened the first aid box and found Tylenol, shook two out and made Joe swallow them.

"I want you to help me," Jenni said to her.

Kim nodded.

"Kim and I are going out for a while, Joe," Jenni said, speaking clearly. "When we come back we're going to clean that wound and check you out, and if I think you need the ER we'll take you."

"We can't leave him," Kim said. "And where are we going?"

Jenni nodded toward Mark, lying exactly where he had dropped. "His pickup's going to be around here someplace. I'm going out and find it and bring it down. Take Joe through to the back bedroom and sit him up. Don't let him lie down. Put plenty of pillows behind him."

Kim felt dizzy, Jenni pushing her too hard, but she had no option but to follow instructions.

"You might want to put some clothes on, too."

Kim smiled. "You weren't complaining earlier."

"Oh, for God's sake, get a room you two," Joe said.

***

Jenni found Mark's pickup on the hill above the beach, drove down and parked as close to the house as possible. When she went inside Joe was sitting up on the single bed in the small downstairs bedroom. Kim had removed his trunks and he lay naked on top of the covers, Ami cuddled against his uninjured side, dropping off to sleep again, all the excitement too much for her.

"Don't get any ideas," he said, as Jenni came in.

"Damn. Kim, come help me get Mark into the pickup."

Between them they dragged Mark outside and somehow managed to push him into the passenger seat. Jenni climbed behind the wheel and pulled the door shut, noticing how much smoother Mark's pickup was than hers.

"I'm going to try and make this look like an accident," she said through the open window. Kim leaned against the door, her head almost level with Jenni's

"How will you get back?"

"I won't. I'll go home. I'm going to call the cops in the morning and say he didn't come home. They won't take me seriously, because he's always not coming home and they know all about Mark, but it'll cover us."

Jenni started the engine but Kim stayed at the window.

"I've gotta go," Jenni said.

"What about afterwards?" Kim asked.

"What about it?"

"You don't need to stay here anymore, you know."

Jenni looked at her. "I know."

Kim leaned in through the window and kissed her. "See you soon."

Jenni nodded and drove in a big circle across the beach and then bounced up the rough track.

***

Kim checked on Joe. He was sitting up in bed, his head back against a pile of pillows, eyelids starting to droop. Ami lay against his side, a trail of drool running from her mouth along his belly. Kim smiled and lifted her, took her upstairs to her cot. She stood for a long while watching her perfect daughter sleep, and a mix of fear and longing washing through her. She shook herself and went downstairs to start cleaning up. There was a lot of blood on the floor.

***

Jenni drove slowly through town, but it was after six Saturday evening and most of the shops closed early out of season. The restaurants and bars hadn't opened yet or were quiet. She passed through town and headed up Lighthouse Road. After a mile it degenerated into a rough track climbing through short grass where sheep grazed. The track ran another two miles along the long spine of the island and then split in two. The right fork would take her down and across to the structure the road was named after. The left hand track petered out after a quarter mile at a rough pull in where kids came to make out and the occasional fisherman parked before climbing down over rocks to the deep water that ran fast here between the island and the mainland. There were no other cars and Jenni pulled up, left the motor running. Outside the daylight was almost gone, which suited her just fine.

Jenni stepped out and walked around to the passenger side, pushed Mark's body across the seat. It took her ten minutes of straining, pushing, pulling and tugging before she had him sitting behind the wheel. She ducked in and placed his foot on the gas pedal. She didn't suppose it was going to make much difference one way or the other, but she wanted to leave nothing to chance.

Beyond the pull in grass started, running downslope to a sudden drop off where the cliffs fell away. There were two hundred yards of grass. Jenni hoped it was enough.

She turned on the headlights, she was going to have to risk that much. It would have been easier if the pickup was automatic. She sat in the passenger side and released the brake. The pickup started to roll slowly forward. There was a low ridge around the edge of the pull in which would stop progress if she let it, so as soon as the truck was moving Jenni pulled the gear stick into second. It fought back, grinding because no-one was depressing the clutch, but finally the gear crashed home and she felt their speed increase. The front wheels hit the edge of the pull in and the steering wheel rocked, came back straight. Now they were running over short grass directly toward the cliff. Jenni glanced at Mark to make sure he was still in position and a scream rose in her throat. His eyes were open and he was staring back at her.

"Where are we going, sweetheart?" he asked, his voice completely rational. "I must have tied a good one on, I don't even know where we are."

Jenni froze in the passenger seat. He was supposed to be dead. She had checked, he *was* dead.

Mark turned his head to the front and stared without comprehension at the approaching cliff edge. Jenni suddenly pulled herself together, saw how close they were to the drop off. She fumbled for the door handle, found it without looking and pushed herself backward as hard as she could. She dropped on the grass, rolling away. The vehicle picked up speed, moving faster, weaving slightly as the front wheels caught hummocks and dips in the grass. The pickup was twenty feet from the cliff edge when the brake lights came on.

Jenni stood, cursing. She ran at the pickup, placed her hands against the tailgate and added her small effort to its progress. The brake lights went out, as though Mark was still unaware of the danger ahead, and the vehicle lost weight beneath Jenni's hands. She stopped, watching as the front wheel hit a small rock on the cliff edge. The pickup jerked to one side and the right front wheel hung out over the edge. The brake lights flared again and the truck hesitated, rocking. The other front wheel dropped, the pickup tilted and even if Mark had his foot hard on the brake no wheels touched the ground now to slow him. There was a grinding as the underside ran across granite, and then the vehicle was gone.

Jenni stood breathing hard, heard a crunch as the pickup hit something on the way down, then another louder crash. She walked to the edge of the cliff. The pickup was on its roof, lodged between two jagged spears of rock, right at the edge of the water. The tide was dropping, but Jenni knew the sea around the island well enough to know within three hours it would return to cover the truck completely. It might pluck the vehicle from between the rocks, it might not. Either way if the drop hadn't finished Mark off the water would. She turned and started walking back to town, angling away from the road, taking a direct line back toward the distant lights.

She arrived a little after nine. On the way across the hillside she kept playing over the emotions she thought she ought to be feeling and didn't. She had just helped murder her husband – no, she corrected, she *had* murdered her husband, because he had been alive when he went over the edge. She might have stopped it then, but too many years of his whining voice, too many punches and slaps, too many wasted opportunities had stayed her hand. Had she believed Mark possessed an ounce of humanity she might have felt sorry for him, but she knew that was not the case. All she experienced was relief. Relief and a suppressed hope.

Had Joe and Kim really meant what they said to her?

Jenni was hungry. She scrambled eggs and ate them standing in the kitchen, the house around her different, silent, that tremor of fear which had inhabited it for so long missing now. She washed her plate, smiling as she remembered what had happened the last time she washed a plate. She went to bed and slept without nightmares.

At eight the next morning she rang the sheriff's office and reported Mark had not returned home last night. She heard skepticism in the officer's voice. It was a small town, a small island; they all knew Mark for the drunk he was, and Jenni imagined the man wondering why she cared enough to report him at all. She experienced a momentary flare of anxiety that the call itself might be regarded as suspicious.

"Look, Jen, I'll put word out, and when someone finds him pulled over still drunk I'll call you, okay?"

"Thanks, Harry. I guess he'll turn up, same as always."

"Maybe you'll get lucky, Jen. Maybe this time he won't."

Jenni hoped her laugh didn't sound forced.

Sunday was her day for washing and she lugged the big checked bags into the back of her pickup and drove to the laundry. She was a regular, and Annie had kept her usual machine free. Jenni spent the next three hours wrapped in steam and heat, folded sheets, pillowcases and towels and dragged them all back home where she would spend the afternoon ironing.

She kept expecting the phone to ring but it remained silent. At just after four Jenni heard a knock at the door and when she opened it Harry Jacobs stood on the step with his hat in his hands and the face Jenni guessed he had worn a few dozen times before.

Chapter 17

They found Mark's body inside the cab of his pickup. People were sympathetic, but Jenni read the truth in their eyes, read what they really thought – she was lucky to be free, lucky Mark had finally gotten drunk enough to fuck up big time.

Jenni was surprised how little emotion she experienced – no, not strictly true – she had no sense of loss, no sense of shame or guilt. What she did feel was a lightness in her soul. Freedom.

Three days after the news broke Jenni had Mark's remains interred in the small island cemetery, strictly reserved for those who had been born on the island. The minister asked in hushed tones if Jenni wanted to reserve a plot beside Mark for her own use, not that she was going to need it for years yet, of course, but one had to think about these things in advance. Jenni suppressed an almost overpowering urge to laugh out loud, trembling as she kept everything buttoned up. The minister, taking her set face and the tremor in her hands for grief patted her knee. Jenni was wearing a short dress and the minister's hand remained a moment too long on her leg.

No, Jenni said, finally able to speak, no need to reserve a plot, telling him she was unsure she was staying around.

When Jenni next went to the beach the Bradford house was all closed up, but a note had been pushed under the door of Kate and Tim's place. Jenni opened the sealed cream envelope, found a note from Kim telling her she had taken Joe back to New York. He was fine, but she wanted a doctor to check out his shoulder. Kim had listed their New York address and three telephone numbers, a landline and two cell phones, as well as an email address. The note finished with a short statement: *We love you. We all love you. Come when you are ready.*

Jenni folded the note back into the envelope and pushed it in the back pocket of her jeans, stripped her clothes off and stood naked in the living room where she had fucked Paul and stared out at the beach. The sand lay deserted in both directions, the day ending, and behind the dunes the sun had already set. Darkness gathered and flowed toward the land over the water. Jenni turned, looked at her mismatched bikini sitting on the chair. She smiled, walked out the door without picking it up and ran down to the surf. The cold water was good against her body, against her breasts, and she stroked out far beyond the breakers, pushing herself hard until she ached deep inside and then she floated on her back and laughed.

When she returned full dark had crept over the beach. Jenni showered and dried, returned to the shadowed living room and lay naked on the couch and made herself come, using her fingers to tease herself, touching her breasts and nipples, stroking her hand along her belly and thighs, eventually pushing four fingers deep between her legs, thinking of Kim and Joe when she finally climaxed, shuddering and crying out.

Days passed and became weeks. Jenni returned to the beach every day as September edged into October, always at the end of the day as dark fell, and on every day but one the beach was deserted and she swam naked, reveling in the water against her skin, and when she came out she repeated the pleasuring of herself, returning home content. Not happy yet, because she was still working out what she was going to do, still working out what happiness meant to her. Although a certainty was starting to grow inside.

One of Mark's buddies, Pete Simpson, surprised her one day by calling and asking if he could take over the repair shop. He could pay a little every month if Jenni was happy with the arrangement. Three weeks after the funeral and Jenni thought he considered it a long enough interval to raise the topic. He also made sure she knew he was available if she wanted someone to share her bed. Pete was married, and Jenni liked his wife. She told him he could have the business, made it clear that was all he could have.

The year dipped into those gray, dark mid-winter days. Jenni spent Thanksgiving and Christmas alone even though her brother had invited her to the west coast for the celebrations.

On New Year day she lugged a suitcase out her front door and locked the house, took her rusty old pickup into town and stopped on the main street, walked into Mary Andrews realty shop.

"Hey, Jen, you've been a stranger."

"I want you to put the house on the market." Jenni sat on the soft leather chair across from Mary's desk, dropped the bunch of keys on the polished surface.

Mary stared at her. They had been good friends once, a long time ago, before Mark started deciding who Jenni could be friends with. Mary was three years older than Jenni, married with two kids and a husband who was devoted to them all.

"Where you going?" Mary not attempting to talk her out of anything.

"Not sure yet. Away."

"I don't know how much you'll get for the place. Is there anything outstanding?"

"Free and clear. The insurance paid everything off. And I don't mind what you get. I don't want to live here anymore."

Mary steepled her fingers, elbows on the desktop, and Jenni wondered what she was seeing. Not a grieving widow, for sure.

"You want coffee while we work this out?"

"Sure."

An hour later Jenni parked the pickup at the harbor and sat outside waiting for the ferry. Ten minutes before five. She wouldn't have long to wait and she watched the gulls fight over scraps from the fishing boats, the odor of rotting fish drifting over her but she hardly noticed; the smell defined this side the island and she had grown used to it.

At a quarter after five she stood at the rail as the ferry pulled out. Jenni looked ahead toward the mainland. She didn't glance back once at what she was leaving.

***

Jenni knew she should have called first, but had been too scared. As she stepped from the cab in front of the apartment block across from Central Park a surge of nerves ran through her. Before she could change her mind she paid the cab and lugged her small suitcase to the wide glass doors. A doorman nodded and opened the door for her. Inside Jenni was directed to the twentieth floor. The elevator opened on a small entrance lobby with a single door. Jenni pressed the buzzer and waited. She waited a minute then pressed the buzzer again.

Should have called, she thought once more.

She tried a third time, the nerves replaced by uncertainty. She was turning away when the door swung wide and Kim came out and hugged her.

"Fuck Jen, you sure took your time girl." Kim kissed her, not the kiss of a friend meeting up after an absence, but the kiss of a lover promising more.

"I wasn't sure whether to call."

"You look gorgeous. Come in."

Jenni followed Kim into a wide hallway. At the far end a dark oak door stood open to a large living room, tall windows facing out over the park.

"Drop your bag, babe, and come through. This deserves a drink."

"You're drinking?" Jenni asked.

Kim laughed. "I tried to keep going as long as I could, but in the end Ami wanted more than I could supply."

As they entered the airy room Jenni saw Ami standing inside a wooden playpen, standing with her fists gripping the bars. When she caught sight of Jenni her face broke into a huge grin.

"Ah-ah-ahh!" she shouted.

"She's missed you," Kim said.

"I've missed her too. Missed you all," Jenni said, getting it out before her courage deserted her. "How's Joe now?"

"Joe's good. But he's not here. He's on that book tour."

"He's well enough for that?"

"So he says. You know he never listens to anything I saw to him. I wanted him to cry off but she said he had to go. And they fixed his shoulder up fine, so there was no reason to postpone." While she spoke Kim poured a glass of white wine for them both, handed one to Jenni.

When Kim's eyes locked onto hers Jenni knew it was going

to be okay and her shoulders relaxed.

"Ah-ahh-ah!" Ami shouted, still waiting to be picked up. She rattled the bars of her playpen.

Kim touched Jenni's arm, closing her fingers around her wrist. "Come here a minute."

Jenni put her wine glass down on the glass table and followed Kim back into the hallway, down a side corridor. Kim stopped and turned to her. Jenni stood in front of Kim, close.

"I didn't want to do this in front of Ami," Kim said, and pulled Jenni close and kissed her, pulling her face down onto hers, one hand sliding down to cup Jenni's ass.

Kim's small breasts pressed against her own, Jenni's nipples instantly hardening to sharp peaks and wetness flooded between her legs. She breathed in the scent of the woman she had thought of ten times a day for the last four months, tasted the sweetness of her lips, fought with her tongue as they both tried to invade each other's mouth and Jenni placed her hand over Kim's breast and felt her arousal too. They ground their hips against each other. Kim kissed her neck, grasped her breasts and lowered her face to them.

"I've missed you, Jen." Kim was breathing hard as she stepped back. She had cut her hair shorter, showing the lobes of her ears. It suited her, Jenni thought, showing more of her face.

"Not as much as I've missed you all."

"Yeah?" Kim grinned.

"Yeah."

"For real?"

"For real."

"You staying?"

"Can I?"

"Fuck yeah."

"Then I'm staying."

Kim kissed her again, briefly ran the flat of her hand down from Jenni's neck, over her breasts, along her belly and finally between her legs. Jenni responded, pressing onto the hand.

From back in the living room Ami's cries grew louder.

"You're going to have to go play with her, you know that."

Jenni nodded, kissed Kim on the neck.

"She usually goes down just after seven," Kim said.

"Yeah?" Jenni's voice sounded hoarse in her ears. "What time is it now?"

Kim laughed and slapped her butt. "Soon, babe, real soon."

***

Jenni lifted Ami out of her playpen, surprised at how much heavier she was, spent an hour rolling around the smooth wooden floor with her, tickling her stomach, sliding her along on her little ass while she laughed and giggled.

Some time later Kim asked, "D'you want to eat, Jen?"

Jenni looked up and shook her head. "Not food."

"You okay with her for a while? I'm gonna grab a shower."

"Sure. Can I feed her?"

"Knock yourself out. She's due any time now, but I'll be out soon if you want to wait. If you really want to everything's in the kitchen, through there."

Jenni played some more, then carried Ami through and heated a jar of food and spent a delightful ten minutes leading the spoon in her hand. Ami had caught on fast and by the time Kim returned in a long silk robe Ami's face was almost clean.

"If you want to clean up I'll finish up here," Kim said, trailing her fingers along Jenni's shoulder. She had applied perfume, expensive and subtle. Beneath Jenni caught the scent of Kim's arousal, too strong to mask.

Jenni went through, searching the corridors until she found a large bathroom where Kim had obviously showered. She looked through a second door and discovered a bedroom. An enormous bed with covers turned down, waiting. Jenni stripped and showered, stepped out and opened the mirrored cabinet, found what she was looking for and stepped back into the shower. She lathered herself and placed the razor flat below her navel, smiled and drew it straight down, removing a band of hair all the way to her clitoris. She repeated the movement until every trace of hair had been removed. She rinsed, enjoying the pulse of the shower against her clitoris, then shaved again, wanting to be as smooth and perfect as she could be. It would have been better with Joe as well, but she was so aroused she didn't think it was going to matter too much whether there were two or three or ten of them.

She turned the shower off and ducked back into the hall and pulled her suitcase through, flicked the catches and took out the garment she had carefully laid on the top of everything else. She shook the sheer jersey dress once and pulled it over her head, wriggled the soft material down over her breasts and belly and hips. She had put on a little weight since September and the dress was even more obscene than the last time she wore it. Which suited Jenni just fine.

When she walked through Kim and Ami were sitting on the wide couch reading a story book. Kim held Ami's hand and traced Ami's finger across each word as she spoke aloud. As she read a word she plopped Ami's fingertip at the start of the word, waited, swishing her finger across as she uttered the word. Each time Ami laughed.

"Dog…" Laugh. "Cat…" Laugh. "Tree…" Laugh.

Kim glanced up, did a double take when she recognized what Jenni wore. Jenni flushed, her nipples hardening instantly.

"Wow!" Kim said, and Ami laughed again, thinking it was a new word.

"You like?"

Kim nodded. She still wore the silk robe, now parted over her legs, showing slim thighs encased in red stockings. They stopped near the top of her thighs and Jenni saw pale flesh above. She sat in a leather armchair across from the couch and watched, waiting as Kim continued to read. The jersey dress rode high on her thighs and she relaxed, comfortable to display for Kim, knowing Ami was too young to care. It was obvious Kim's attention was no longer on the book, and Ami sensed this as well and after five minutes her eyes began to droop.

"I'm going to put her down," Kim said.

Jenni nodded. "Can I come?" She followed Kim to a pretty nursery, animal prints on the walls, revolving mobiles hanging from the ceiling. Kim laid Ami in her cot, kissed her pretty face and stood while they both watched her drift into sleep. Jenni stood beside Kim, their fingers lightly brushing, conscious of heat radiating from her body.

When Ami was asleep Kim said, "So… what d'you feel like doing now?"

Jenni shrugged. "You wanna go out somewhere?"

Kim laughed and took her hand. "Fuck that."

Jenni kicked the bedroom door closed behind them. Kim checked she could hear Ami breathing on the baby monitor then let the robe slip from her shoulders and pool on the wood floor. She stood with her back to Jenni dressed in red stockings, minute red panties and red bra. Jenni walked over and slipped her arms around from behind, cupping Kim's breasts.

"Know what I really want to do?"

"Same as me?" Kim said.

Jenni nodded and kissed Kim's shoulder.

Kim turned inside her arms and they kissed.

"I just love you in that dress, Jen, but d'you think we can take it off now?"

Jenni let Kim work the dress upward. As it revealed her cleanly shaved pussy Kim stopped, leaned in and kissed her there, her lips and tongue electric on Jenni's skin.

"I like," Kim said.

"D'you still shave yourself?" Jenni asked.

"Why d'you think I was so long in the shower, babe?" She kissed Jenni again.

"If you don't stop doing that I think I'm gonna come right here and now."

Kim kissed her again. "Good."

Jenni grabbed her and pulled her up. "Not yet." Jenni pulled the dress over her head and tossed it aside. "Now you're overdressed."

"Fix that for me." Kim turned her back and Jenni unclipped the bra. Jenni went to her knees and slid her fingers up inside the tight panties, her palms flat against Kim's ass. Her thumb probed between Kim's cheeks and found her budded rear entrance.

"Oh fuck, babe, you don't mess around, do you?"

Jenni kissed her hip, started to ease the panties down.

"No – tear 'em off," Kim gasped, her breath coming fast.

"But they're–"

"Tear 'em," Kim growled, and Jenni gripped the fine silk and pulled hard. They tore down the back, parted and hung loose on Kim's hips. Kim turned around, presenting herself to Jenni and she needed no encouragement. She reached up, her hands on Kim's breasts and her mouth closed around Kim's clitoris and drew it against her tongue.

Kim gripped Jenni's hair in her fist and held her against her before pulling away. She walked backward until her legs met the bed, allowed herself to fall back, parting her thighs, staring down at Jenni, making her need obvious.

Jenni slipped her tongue along Kim's smooth thighs and invaded her sweet entrance. Fluid met her tongue, sweet and scented of Kim. Jenni wanted more. She pushed Kim along the bed, straddled her, grabbing Kim's legs and body and turning her, pressing her own soaking pussy down against hers, grunting as she began to ride against the lighter woman. Jenni's deep breasts swayed and bounced, her head going back. Kim reached up and touched her, trying to reach everywhere at once. Jenni leaned forward, her belly touching Kim's belly, her breasts trembling against Kim's breasts, her pussy flattened to Kim's pussy and she fucked her, hard and relentless, watching the fire peak in Kim's eyes once and her body tremored against her own and still Jenni ground against her, grabbed her and turned Kim over and locked her legs back around her, pussy now against Kim's ass and she fucked her like that, fucked her hard and desperately until Kim cried out a second time and Jenni gripped her hips tight and fucked her until her own climax peaked and erupted.

"Yes, babe... fuck me," Kim grunted.

Jenni heaved against her, the fire almost too much to bear and when she came she gushed hard against Kim's ass, her fluids soaking Kim and dripping down onto the covers.

They lay wrapped together, unable to exist for more than a minute without kissing, unable to resist touching each other.

"I've decided I like fucking girls," Kim said.

"Good. 'Cause I haven't near finished with you yet."

"Ooh, tell me. Tell me what you're gonna do to me."

"Everything."

Kim laughed. "Not enough. You going to squirt like that every time?"

"I've never come like that before."

"I liked it."

"Me too."

"I've made a mess all over your bed."

Kim kissed her nipple, spent some time playing with both breasts and Jenni lay on her back, luxuriating in another woman's hands on her body, a vibration starting up inside.

"Make as much mess as you like, babe," Kim said, coming up to kiss her lips. "Someone else can wash 'em now."

Jenni laughed and pulled Kim up until her mouth found her soft pussy, tugging Kim's legs so her knees straddled her shoulders, holding Kim against her as she tried to work free, showing no mercy until Kim climaxed against her and slumped back, loose and tangled against Jenni.

Kim twisted and turned to lie flat on Jenni, their bodies fitting together.

"What's Joe going to think when he gets home?" Jenni asked, nervous again.

"Same as me," Kim said.

"Are you sure?"

Kim lifted herself up on her arms, glanced down across Jenni and nodded. "Oh yeah, babe. Just look at you. He's going to love this."

Jenni was in free-fall, wind rushing past. She had stepped off the edge, trusting to fate, trusting to this couple she was madly in love with.

Chapter 18

It was Jenni's first time in an airplane, and she had chosen to break herself in on a long-haul flight. The entire experience was new to her, the freshness of it all swamping any nerves she had, fascinated at every step of the process. She even enjoyed the queue to pass through security. Had she possessed a passport before coming to New York she would have been taking this flight sooner, but she had been forced to wait while her application was processed. Kim had helped Jenni complete the forms.

Now, forty thousand feet over the Atlantic west of Ireland the pilot came on and announced in the voice Jenni was already recognizing as *the pilot voice* that they would shortly be crossing over the south west tip of Ireland and if they looked through the left side windows they would catch a glimpse of Cork. Jenni was sitting in a window seat, but on the other side. There was a name other than left or right, and although Jenni remembered the names she couldn't remember which was which. Right side window suited her fine. She gazed down for the first hour before becoming bored at cloud and Atlantic. She slept, woke for lunch, read – not one of Joe's books but a Steven King which had been signed and sent to Joe in return for one of his. Jenni had not wanted to bring the book, even though she did like Steven King's writing. Kim had insisted she had to, could not leave the book a quarter read, the book that had sat on the nightstand on the left side of the bed. The bed she had shared with Kim every night since arriving in New York.

Fifteen minutes later Jenni caught sight of land through her window and the big Boeing shuddered slightly as thermals rose at the border between water and earth. Her ears popped as they started a long descent. The pilot came back on and told them they would be arriving ahead of schedule at three-forty. The seat belt signs came on and they were asked to put their seat backs up. Jeni's had been up throughout the flight. She hadn't wanted to miss anything.

As they descended the landscape came up to meet them. Jenni made out houses, roadways, traffic on highways although Kim had told her they were called motorways over here. Lots of houses, lots of roads, many cars. A small country, the entire British Isles able to fit inside some American states with room to spare, but only if you flattened it down a little first.

Jenni noticed some of the passengers around her gripping their armrests as the big plane came down and the land streamed backward past the window, but she felt only excitement. They crossed a wide roadway packed with traffic, some driver craning their heads up, so close Jenni felt she could reach out and touch them. Then they were crossing the outer boundary and suddenly wheels touched. The plane bounced once, gently, came back and stuck. The nose dipped and the engines roared as panels came out to deflect their blast. G-force pushed Jenni forward and she grinned, so many new experiences. She glanced at her watch, the old one with the scratched face she had been given by her brother as a wedding present. Ten after three. By the time they taxied and the doors were opened another fifteen minutes had passed. Jenni was one of the first through the door. She had nothing other than a small bag stored in the overhead locker. She stowed the book carefully inside, determined not to lose it even though Kim had laughed at her fears.

"Fuck, Jen, we'll just get Steve to sign another if you lose it!"

Getting out of the airport was simpler than getting in had been and by four Jenni was waiting for a train. She could have taken a cab, Kim said money was not an issue. Jenni had so far refused to take anything off Kim and Joe. She had her own money. Her small house had sold faster than she expected, bought by off-islanders looking for a vacation bolt hole. Wrong side of the island, but they wouldn't know that yet. Jenni had enough money of her own for the moment. She had bought her own ticket, could afford a cab but she and Kim had sat at the laptop and discovered the train was the fastest way into central

London.

Thursday in February, light already fading from the sky, the weather warmer than Jenni had expected as the train whisked her into Paddington station. From there she did take a cab, giving the driver the address she had written on a slip of paper. The last leg made her the most nervous. She had to be at her destination by six. Any later and the whole plan would be blown. And trying to get across London at five in the evening was, apparently, a lot harder than she had imagined.

Jenni leaned forward and spoke through the open glass partition. Ahead of the cab stationery traffic had not moved in five minutes.

"I really need to be at that address before six. Is there anything you can do? It's worth a good tip if you get me there on time."

The driver's eyes met hers in the mirror.

"See what I can do, love." He didn't sound at all like Dick van Dyke. His voice was the real deal. "As soon as we can move an inch."

Jenni slumped back. Checked her watch. Five-forty.

Another five minutes passed before the traffic started to move.

"This town's a nightmare, love."

Jenni nodded. Town?

The driver cut his black cab right across traffic, raising a blast of horns, ducked into an alley that looked too narrow but he barreled straight in, hung a hard left and right, dipped down beneath an archway, back up and bullied his way into another stream of traffic. Two minutes passed and he repeated the maneuver. He was grinning, enjoying himself.

"I'll get you there in plenty of time, love, don't you worry."

They pulled up outside Foyles bookshop in Charring Cross Road at ten before six.

Jenni pulled a fifty pound note from her wallet and pushed it through to the driver. "Is this enough?"

"Too much, love. I'll get your change."

"Keep it." She was already climbing out.

"I hope he's worth it."

Jenni stopped long enough to reply. "Oh, he is." Then she was standing on the sidewalk as people streamed around her, looking at Joe's picture on a poster in the bookshop window. Written in large black letters: February 13th - Personal appearance by Joe Fransiscus signing his number one bestseller *Dead Time*.

Jenni pushed through the door.

"Where's the signing?" she asked a man stacking books into a display. He pointed through to the back of the store and Jenni wound her way through bookcases and display stands.

Her watch showed five before six and she couldn't see him anywhere. She swung around, went back the way she had come, tried another direction, panic fluttering in her chest. She wished Kim had come with her, but she never flew unless she absolutely had to, and beside Ami needed her at home.

"Don't you worry?" Jenni has asked as they lay in bed together, naked as they always were, sated after making love, legs and arms tangled.

"Worry about what?"

"Me going to Joe. Don't you worry I might run away with him?"

Kim laughed. "Why would you want to do that?"

"I don't know. But aren't you jealous?"

"Mm-mm, not me." Kim shook her head, slid her hand onto Jenny's stomach. "I *know* you don't want to give this up, babe." She kissed Jenni and five minutes later Jenni was sitting astride her face, her tongue deep inside Kim's pussy as they worked slowly on bringing each other to a third climax of the day.

No, Jenni thought, I won't give this up.

If Kim had come they would have found Joe. Now Jenni's watch showed three minutes off six and she swung around a big display stand, moving wildly now, without a plan and saw Joe across a space. A bench was piled high with copies of his book and three people remained in the queue as he took a book from each one, spoke quietly with them, shook hands, and signed their copy.

Jenni grabbed one of Joe's books and joined the end of the

queue.

Two people. One. Then she stood in front of him. He reached out without looking up and Jenni placed the book in his hand.

"Who shall I make it out to?"

His voice cut through her, making her melt inside.

"Jenni."

She saw Joe smile. "I know someone with the same-" His voice stopped dead as he looked up, recognizing her voice. His mouth dropped open and the book fell onto the desk with a thud.

"Aren't you going to sign it?"

"Uh…"

"Well, in that case." Jenni crossed her arms, made to turn away.

"What the fuck are you doing here? Why? When? Shit, Jen, it's good to see you. What?" Joe shook his head and Jenni laughed. It had been killing her the last few weeks because Kim had spoken with Joe but not mentioned Jenni turning up in New York.

"We're gonna keep it a surprise," Kim has said.

Now Joe looked past Jenni. "Just you?"

Jenni nodded. "Just me."

"When did you get here?"

"About an hour ago."

"Wow."

"You going to sign that or not? I used to have a signed Joe Fransiscus, but someone burned it. I'd sure like another one."

"In that case." Joe opened the book and scrawled inside, not allowing Jenni to see the inscription, but she knew already what he had written. "Are you staying?"

"I don't know. I haven't got anywhere booked."

Joe laughed. "I might be able to find a spare room at my hotel."

"Maybe they're full."

"Maybe. I guess you might have to share with me if that's the case."

"I do hope they're full."

Joe glanced beyond her. "You're the last one. Come on, let's get out of here." He stood and came around the desk, put his arm around Jenni and kissed her, tentative at first as though she might have changed her mind about him. Jenni kissed him back hard, letting her tongue into his mouth, making sure Joe know she hadn't.

Joe took her hand. As they turned an assistant was standing watching them with a puzzled expression.

"Would you like a photo with Mr. Fransiscus, madam?"

Jenni laughed. "No, I don't think so."

"Oh."

Jenni made to walk past the woman but she put her hand on Jenni's arm. Jenni stopped.

"You need to pay for your book, madam."

Jenni laughed. Joe joined in, tears in both their eyes they were laughing so hard and the book shop assistant had no idea what she had said that was so funny.

***

Joe closed the door of his room as Jenni walked ahead. This was more than a room, this was a suite, with a living room looking out over busy streets.

"You want something to eat, drink?"

Jenni turned back to him, nervous. "Nothing."

Joe crossed half the distance between them, stopped. Jenni realized she wasn't the only nervous one.

"How have you been, Jen?"

She nodded. "Good. How's the shoulder?"

He shrugged, lifting his arm. "That's good too." Joe took another two paces. Stopped again. Three feet separated them now and Jenni caught his scent, the essence of Joe, unchanged from months ago, her body responding.

"D'you think I could use your shower?" Jenni felt grubby from the flight, didn't want to get close to Joe, sure she smelled bad.

"On one condition."

"Yeah?"

Joe nodded.

"What condition's that?" Jenni felt her stomach trembling. It was going to be okay.

"I can wash your back."

Jenni shook her head, suppressing a smile at the puppy dog expression on Joe's face. "My front's dirty too, Joe. I need more than my back scrubbing."

Joe's cock showed thick inside his pants and this time Jenni took the steps, closing the gap between them to nothing.

"How have you really been, Jen?" His breath covered her face.

"I'll tell you all about it, Joe, but first I need you to fuck me. It's okay, Kim knows."

"She does?"

Who d'you think talked me into this?"

"That Kim," Joe said.

Jenni nodded. "Yeah, that Kim." Her fingers were stroking his cock through his pants and her knees went weak. She wanted him so much.

Joe turned her around and unzipped her dress, slid it from her shoulders. His fingers fumbled with the clasp on her bra but Jenni refused to help, waiting until he unclipped her. The bra clung against her breasts and she let it stay while Joe's fingers found her panties and pulled them down. His lips touched her back, her ass, her thighs.

"I really do need a shower, Joe," she said, her voice low.

"You smell great."

"I don't think I do."

"You do to me. Besides, I can't wait."

She turned to him, letting him see her shaved pussy, letting his mouth close over her clitoris and suddenly her knees went and she fell to the floor, her bra finally releasing its kiss from her breasts. Joe leaned over her and she said, "Take your clothes off Joe and fuck me right here, right now, any way you want."

Joe sat back and unbuttoned his shirt, tore at his pants and shorts. Jenni twisted, grabbing for his cock while he still fumbled with his shoes and socks, wriggled close and took him inside her mouth, the remembrance of his taste flooding her, the remembrance of his body raising gooseflesh along her arms and legs. Joe gave up on his shoes and lay back, his pants and shorts rucked around his ankles and Jenni took his cock deeper, took it to the root, the thick ridged head sliding into her throat and Joe cried out and came instantly, a flood of semen filling her mouth and she let it pool and slip between her lips.

"Oh fuck, Jen, I'm sorry. That was so…"

She waited and then climbed along him, kissed him, knowing his cum coated her lips. Joe kissed her back, his hands on her body.

"Don't worry, babe." She reached down. "You're still hard."

"Oh God, Jen. I'm dreaming. I got to be dreaming."

"Mm – good dream."

"The best."

Jenni stroked his cock, slid back down and pecked the tip with a kiss, kept going and untied his shoes and finally released the tangle of clothes from his ankles.

She stood and walked naked, tall and slim, knowing how good she looked, confident and assured now, no longer beaten down. She sat on the edge of the couch, knowing the windows were behind her and not caring. They might be too high up for anyone to see what they were going to do, but she didn't care if they did. She beckoned Joe with her finger and he stood and came to her, his long thick cock swaying from side to side with each step.

He knelt between her legs and kissed the smooth shaved skin above her pussy.

"Kim did this to you?"

"Of course."

"I like."

"Me too."

"I think I can last a bit longer this time," Joe said, and Jenni laughed.

Joe sat back. "What?"

"Nothing, honey. You reminded me of someone else, that's all."

Joe frowned, but Jenni knew he wouldn't stay puzzled long. "I want you to fuck me now, Joe. My turn."

He slid along her, kissing her thighs, heading towards her pussy. Jenni twisted her fingers in his hair and pulled him up, shaking her head. "No, I don't need that. I've been waiting for this too long already. Just fuck me, Joe."

He let her pull him up but Jenni released him and slid down off the couch underneath him. She sucked his cock, licked his balls, turned so her legs were raised on the cushions of the couch and her pussy presented beneath his cock. She looked up along his back, put her hands on his ass, feeling the muscle beneath the skin. She twisted her body, tendon and muscle loose and she could contort herself into almost any position. She wanted to surprise Joe, wanted to delight him.

"I want to be fucked like this," she said and Joe pushed his cock down against her, the head finding her slit and Jenni rocked so he entered her an inch. Joe shifted back and Jenni touched his asshole and felt him twitch, then he was filling her and she closed her eyes and breathed hard as his rigid thickness opened her cunt walls, so slick and wet and she had no idea why she had wanted this position but found Joe could fill her completely, felt the head of his cock touch her cervix and she came hard and fast, instantly tipping over, grinding up against Joe, her finger pushing hard and invading his asshole, crying out as the world spun away, grayed out and only slowly returned.

When she came back Joe still filled her, twisting round to look at her, his hands reaching back to caress her breasts.

"I'm not the only one around here comes fast," he said.

Jenni laughed. She pushed him, his cock slipping from her, emptiness ready for something else. She had promised Kim she would do this for Joe, while they lay together in bed, playing with each other.

A week after Jenni moved in Kim had come to bed, shy for once and when Jenni pressed her she said she wanted to try something but didn't know if Jenni was up for it.

Anything, Jenni said, you know that.

Kim had left the bed, came back with something in her hand, Jenni laughing with glee when she saw a dildo and straps for securing it.

"You or me?" Jenni asked.

"Me first," Kim said.

"Me after?"

"If you want."

"Want."

Now it was Joe's turn. Jenni rolled onto her front, grabbed a pillow and stuffed it underneath her so her ass was lifted. She raised one leg and stuck it out to one side.

"You know what I want, Joe."

"Fuck, Jen." He stared at her, not believing.

"I like being fucked in the ass, Joe. I like it a lot."

"Did... did Mark..."

Jenni laughed. "Never. But others have. Fuck me, Joe, fuck me now."

"Oh God." Joe's voice was strangled. He sounded lost and Jenni smiled, knowing how much he wanted this. She felt his weight against her back, his mouth on her parted ass, his tongue.

I should have taken that shower, she thought, but Joe didn't seem to care, his tongue invading her tightness, wetting her, rippling thrills deep into her core and Jenni thought she might come again before he used his cock, but Joe couldn't wait either and when she was wet he lay against her, his thigh pressed against the cheek of her ass, the head of his cock touching her, applying pressure. Jenni parted herself wider, feeling the pressure build. She enjoyed this, had enjoyed it since the first time, gasping as Joe's cock opened her asshole and slipped inside, the sense of fullness in her belly.

"Stop me if I-"

"You won't," Jenni said. "I want all of it, Joe."

"Jen."

He let his weight press against her and Jenni felt his cock invade her further, deeper, filling her completely until Joe's pubic hair pressed hard against her ass and she felt him start to thrust. She lifted herself up, trying to get him deeper and Joe reached around and held her breast, dropped his hand to her belly, back to her breast.

Jenni was fulfilled, knowing how much this meant to Joe, knowing how much she wanted him. She was going to let Joe fuck her like this for Kim when they returned home. She grinned, pushed back against Joe, his stomach against her ass. Home, she thought. When we go home.

Joe was moving faster, his cock sliding almost all the way from her ass then burying deep as he came back down. Jenni felt a tremble start inside and knew she was going to come, made no effort to stop it, writhing beneath Joe as her second climax ripped through her and when she came out the other side Joe was still fucking her and she came up onto hands and knees and let him grip her hips. She felt her breasts swaying, reached a hand up and touched herself, reached down along her belly and found her clitoris with her thumb, pushed two fingers inside her pussy, feeling Joe's cock through the thin layer of skin beneath her pussy, felt him huge and vibrant inside.

"Jen – oh fuck, Jen!" Joe cried out and Jenni felt his seed spill into her, a long outpouring hosing deep inside and she rammed her fingers into her pussy and came again, shaking hard, sweat popping along her throat. Her legs and the one hand could not hold her up any longer and she slumped onto the floor. Joe followed, staying inside, lying across her, taking his weight on his elbows, kissing her shoulders and neck.

They lay for long minutes, breathing hard, then breathing softly.

"Does this mean you're going to stay, Jen?"

She laughed beneath him. "I guess so."

"Good. You okay with all this?"

"Guess."

"Mm... I guess you are."

"You and Kim got room for one more, Joe?"

"You bet."

Jenni smiled, the warmth of him covering her.

"I think I really do need that shower now, Joe."

"I still want to scrub your back."

"Of course"

"Are you staying?" Joe stopped on his way to the bathroom, tall and slim, the scar showing on his shoulder.

"If I can."

"Two more weeks," Joe said.

Jenni nodded.

They had those two weeks together as Joe finished his tour, boarded their flight back to New York and a stewardess stopped Joe as he stepped onto the plane and asked if he was Joe Fransiscus the writer. When he said he was she directed them left into an almost empty first class. Joe signed copies of his books for the entire crew and somewhere over mid Atlantic even the pilot came back to shake his hand and chat. Jenni realized then how her life was going to be, how different Joe's life was from the one she had known.

Kim and Ami met them at JFK and they took a cab back into the city.

Chapter 19

Joe sat at his desk in front of the big picture window that looked across central park and turned on his MacBook. While waiting he closed his eyes and remembered sitting on his grandmother's knee. He could have been no older than five or six, but the memory was clear of her rolling a sheet of crisp white paper into an old black Royal. The clack of the cogs as she racked paper through, the hard rattle of the keys. She had let him try it out, the effort of putting a letter on paper surprising him. Later there were his first memories of writing on that same typewriter at her house, the short, meaningless stories he created which his grandmother praised despite their faults. Even back then characters and scenes jostled in his head, each calling for attention, each wanting to be the first to be heard. Writing was easier now with the Mac, but sometimes he thought back to that physical act of getting words down, wondered if he could still work that way if he had to, if all the power went out.

He felt full of words, pregnant with them. His last book had sold well, the two months spent touring to promote worthwhile. He was incapable of writing on planes or in hotels so the words had dammed up inside his head, ready to burst loose. Finally the book signings and interviews and tv appearances were over, and he needed to get back to his real job, putting words on a screen. This would be his fifth novel. The second since Jenni had come to live with them.

He opened his eyes and released his thoughts, fingers flying over the keys.

They came to the beach house at the tail end of August, after the season had finished. Driving through town from the ferry Katie said she thought it was too quiet, and Pete said great, they had come here for a rest, not to party. Katie leaned across and kissed his cheek. When she sat back Pete glanced across at her and smiled. At four months, she was just starting to show. This break would be good for her; good for both of them.

"Pete, watch out!" Katie yelled and he glanced up, slamming on the brakes even before he saw what lay in the road. A skinny man wearing a soiled denim jacket stood in the middle of the empty street, weaving slightly, a bottle of cheap whiskey showing from the top of a brown paper bag.

He flipped the bird at them. "What the fuck you think you doing? Fuckin' tourists!"

Joe stopped as slim arms snaked around him. A large belly pressed against his back and he reached around and cupped both hands against a firm ass.

"Is this the new book?" Jenni leaned across to read, nipping his earlobe as she passed, her breasts parting around the back of his neck and Joe responded, as he always did, his cock thickening along his thigh.

"Only an idea at the moment."

"Can I read it?"

"I don't know," Joe said, uneasy.

Jenni picked up the tone in his voice. "If you don't want me to I won't."

"It's not that. I'd like you to. It's just..."

She kissed the top of his head, and from along the hallway Kim called out, asking if they wanted lunch now or later.

"Later," Jenni called back, her fingers tracing the muscle across Joe's chest, finding the line of raised skin that would always be there now. "I won't read it if you don't want me to, babe."

"I do want you to. It's just..." He sighed. "I stopped letting Kim read anything until it was actually in print."

"It's okay, Joe, really."

"I stopped her because she always tries to make it better, and I can't stand that." Joe knew he sounded pathetic and stopped talking.

"I won't do that," Jenni whispered, her breath soft against his ear.

"Pa!" Ami's high voice sounded and Joe heard her bare feet patter across the wooden floor. He turned in his chair, knowing he would have to come back to this later as Ami's grin shattered his heart.

Jenni offered her hand and Ami lifted hers up high to take it.

"Up, Momma," she said, and Jenni leaned and lifted her and rested Ami on her hip, Ami's leg curling over the full bloom of her belly. It seemed as far as Ami was concerned Kim and Jenni were interchangeable, two Moms for the price of one. In a couple of months another voice would join their group, and whatever it was, boy, girl, they didn't want to know, that child would have two Moms as well.

Printed in Great Britain
by Amazon.co.uk, Ltd.,
Marston Gate.